THE MASTER-KNOT OF HUMAN FATE

Adapted by
JENNIFER HURT

From the novel by
Ellis Meredith

Rising Star Visionary Press trade paperback edition: March, 2010

**A Rising Star Visionary Press book
for extra copies please contact by e-mail at
<u>risingstarvisionarypress@earthlink.net</u>
or send by regular mail to
Rising Star Visionary Press
Copies Department
P O Box 9226
Fountain Valley, CA 92728-9226**

<u>www.risingstarvisionarypress.vpweb.com</u>

Loosening the Master-Knot

I read The Master-Knot of Human Fate by Ellis Meredith many, many years ago when I was a young girl. A teacher had assigned it to me as extra credit (or "make-up points" as she called it) for missing school when I had the chicken pox. Thinking the premise sounded boring, I just skimmed it first, determined to get through the assignment... then found myself actually enjoying it, and I re-read it at a slower pace.

I was struck by what a beautiful story it was. The couple stranded in the mountains by a deluge that leaves them in a Robinson Crusoe-dilemma was an exciting idea, but I was touched by the chaste love that grew between them and all of their deep thoughts and discussions. The story remained with me, and I spent time at the library exploring many of the works and philosophies they talked about—something I probably never would have been interested in if not for Ellis Meredith's beautiful work.

Decades later, my granddaughter Melinda discovered the joys of reading thanks to the then-new Twilight series, and I thought that I might share my childhood treasure with her. I dug through an old trunk until I found my beloved, well-read copy, dusted it off, and presented it to her for her birthday.

A couple of months went by, and I finally asked my son, Melinda's father, what she had thought of it. This led to the awkward revelation that she had never been able to get past the first few chapters. While my feelings were not at all hurt, I was a little disappointed, and when the book was returned to me, I decided to re-read it myself... which led to a startling discovery!

Much to my surprise, while I still enjoyed the overall story itself, I found the writing style—particularly the dialogue—very stilted and unnatural! Something I had taken in stride as a young girl had not aged well at all, and since I've been a reader all these years, my reading tastes had evolved with popular styles.

Well, I thought, no wonder Melinda couldn't get into this book! How disappointing.

And yet... I still loved the sentiments behind the work, still wanted to share its deep and heartfelt majesty with my granddaughter.

And so, not knowing the first thing about the "public domain"—and not needing to at that point, since I never intended to publish it!—I set about "translating" the book, particularly the dialogue, into a more modern style. I considered adding some back-story between the two characters, but ultimately decided to leave the plot untouched.

And so, on her next birthday, I re-presented my own version of The Master-Knot of Human Fate to Melinda. And this time, she read and enjoyed it from the first page to the last!

Well, my mission was done as far as I was concerned. This had been done as a gift for Melinda, nothing more. It took some work, but I was seeking no reward beyond a bonding experience with my granddaughter.

But the story didn't stop there. The book—mostly without my knowledge—began circulating through the family, then to family-friends, then to the local middle school where my daughter was a teacher.

This past summer—more than a year after I had given the updated book to Melinda—my daughter told me that she had discussed the it with an old college friend, Lindsey, who was now helping her father run a small publishing house. This publishing house, Rising Star Visionary Press, had apparently released a similarly adapted version of Hamlet and had plans for a Sherlock Holmes adaptation later this year and hopes for a Macbeth in the future... and they were very interested in releasing my version of Master-Knot on a test-market basis.

Well, I was very flattered, of course,

but I assured her that this simply could
not be. After all, I had done this as a
personal project—I certainly didn't own
the rights to the story!

And this, of course, led to my education
about the public domain and, ultimately,
the manuscript you now hold in your hands.

So... here you are, dear reader. I hold
no claim over the original content of the
following story, but I hope you find the
modernized dialogue to your liking. I
wholeheartedly recommend your checking out
the original edition sometime, if you can
embrace the dated text, and seeing for
yourself the building blocks from which I
worked.

And I hope you enjoy this wonderful tale
as much as I and my granddaughter have.

Jennifer Hurt,
October 2009

Up from Earth's Centre through the Seventh Gate
I rose, and on the Throne of Saturn sate,
    And many a Knot unravel'd by the Road;
    But not the Master-knot of Human Fate.
* * * * *
Ah Love! could you and I with Him conspire
To grasp this sorry Scheme of Things entire,
    Would not we shatter it to bits—and then
    Re-mould it nearer to the Heart's Desire!

Omar Khayyâm

I

One spring morning, a man and a woman climbed slowly along one of the most rugged of the many Rocky Mountain trails. The air was cold, and farther up the mountains little patches of snow lay here and there in the hollows. Two or three miles below them nestled one of the most famous pleasure resorts of the entire region; three or four times as far lay the nearest town of any importance. Over the plain and through the clear atmosphere, it looked like a bird's-eye-view map rather than an actual town. Far away to the left, gorgeous in coloring and grotesque in outline, could be seen the odd figures of many strangely piled rocks.

The man and woman stopped now and then to rest and look out over the matchless scene and take in its wonderful beauty. The woman was tall and slender, with a superb posture; even on that steep ascent, she moved with the grace and freedom of one who has entire command of her body. She was also well dressed for such an excursion. Her short, green skirt did not impede her movements, and high, stout shoes gave her firm footing. She had removed her jacket, and in her bright pink silk blouse and abbreviated half-slip, with the glow of the morning on her usually pale face, she looked almost girlish... but her face was not that of girlhood. It was without lines, and the heavy mass of her golden-brown hair remained free of silver or gray; but her white forehead was serene with the calmness that follows overcoming, and her dark gray eyes saw the world disarmed of its illusions. In her there were, or had been, unrealized capacities for life in all its height and depth and breadth. In studying her, one became vaguely aware that, having missed these things, she had found a fourth dimension which compensated for the loss.

Her companion was younger than her by several years, and so much taller that she seemed almost small in comparison. In his eyes there danced and shined the light of truth and courage and hope, and he walked with the buoyancy of joy and youth. He could have served as the model for any of the old gods, and fairly glowed with the exuberance of youth.

The relation between the two was problematic. Certainly there was no question of love on either side. Equally certainly there existed a rare and exquisite camaraderie between them, a perfect comprehension that often made words unnecessary; a mere look sufficed.

They toiled up the steep, narrow path

until they reached a wide trail, a road
that had been laid out, then abandoned. It
swept around the mountainside, miles above
the little city on the plain, and
terminated suddenly at an immense gateway
of stone. Here the mountain had been torn
apart, and two palisades of gray-green rock
rose grim and terrible for hundreds of
feet, while between them, dashing over
boulders and trees, a little stream rushed
along in the eternal shadows at their base.
Beyond a rustic gate, standing across the
path that narrowed to a few feet before the
wall of stone and beneath the intense blue
sky, a park, sparkling and green in the
sunlight, was visible. They stopped and
regarded the two gateways—one the work of
nature; the other the feeble forgery of
Man—and then, swinging open the creaking
wooden affair, passed into the peaceful
valley. A few yards away stood a small log
cabin, but the chimney was smokeless, and
though the chickens clucked in the yard and
a dog, a collie, lay on the doorstep, it
seemed desolate and deserted.

Passing along an almost invisible trail,
they found themselves in the wildest and
most remote part of that wild and remote
region. They saw a few stray animals, but
no human beings. This was one of the few
places where mining was not a universal
pursuit, and it was too early to do much in
the few mines that did exist. There are
entire sections in the Rockies that are

deserted for more than half the year, and this was one of them. That day there was no one at the signal station; the keeper had gone down to the valley for fresh stores, and to learn something of the terrific disturbances that were said to be threatening the entire Eastern coast with annihilation. Perhaps the owners of the log cabin had made a similar pilgrimage.

Now the scene was flooded with moonlight when the travelers passed the gate on their homeward way, and sat down on a boulder a few yards without the frowning portal. The night was cold, and the woman put on her jacket and sank her numbed fingers in its pockets. In spite of her weariness, she was troubled and restless, and, turning, looked first at the overhanging crags behind of them, then away over the plain at the twinkling lights of the town below. They heard indistinctly the sounds of bells ringing wildly, and overhead flocks of birds circled and called with shrill, uncanny voices. Yet the moonlight was so bright that they saw each other as plainly as if it were still day, and its placid radiance seemed strangely at odds with the disturbed wild fowl, and certain weird and fitful sounds that seemed to sigh forth from the bosom of the earth.

"It's a pity," she said, "that we can't pass through this gateway into paradise without descending to earth again."

"I don't believe you are half as tired

of life as you say," he answered with an impatient movement of his head. "You may not cringe from death as I do, or enjoy life as much, but isn't it a good thing to be alive tonight? Isn't it fine to be a mile or so above the rest of humanity and the deadly conventionalities? Aren't you glad you came?"

She did not answer, but presently said dreamily, "Suppose that plain was the sea."

"It isn't hard to suppose," he answered with a smile. "I have seen the Pacific when it looked just like that."

"Oh, no," she said quickly. "Nothing is like the sea but itself. You'll never persuade me that I love the mountains as much. And the plains... just imagine if all that gray-green silver were gray-blue, with here and there a gathering crest of foam, racing to break in spray about these mountains—"

"Why, look," he said, drawing her a little to one side, "there is your liquid blue, with its white crest moving toward us. Could the real sea look more wonderful than that? It's blotting out everything. Now it recedes. Wasn't it real?"

She started to her feet. "This is a very strange night," she said irrelevantly, in a rather strained voice. "Listen, and see how many birds are flying about us; I never saw them fly like this at night. What does it mean?"

They stood together, looking at each other with startled faces. The whole mountain, all the mountains, seemed to be alive and trembling under them. Overhead, thousands of birds wheeled and screamed with terror in their mingled outcries. The little creeping things scuttled away up the mountain. The silver-blue wave widened and spread over the plain from north to south, and the air was full of a dull, terrible roar, as if the fountains of the great deep had broken up, and a thousand white-crested waves rushed toward the hapless city before them. They covered it, and with a wild jangle of bells, faintly audible over the uproar, it sank out of sight, all the gleaming, dancing lights disappearing in an instant. The white crests came on and broke about the mountains, and receded and came on again with a deafening roar. Then the crust of the earth between the mountain range and the spot where the city had been seemed to crack like a dried orange peel and the flood rushed over the abyss, and there arose a blinding steam that hid the whole scene below, and, ascending, circled the mountain peaks in mist.

All around them on the mountainside rose the cries of terrified wild things, and along the narrow pathway into the park, a herd of cattle and horses rushed and disappeared among the aspens that trembled as never before. The collie, scenting their presence, came and crouched whining at their feet. The woman moved through the fog toward the figure of her companion. His arm closed about her convulsively.

"Should we go farther up the mountain?" he asked.

"'If it be now, 'tis not to come; if it be not to come, it will be now,'" she answered, insensibly finding it easier to use another's words than to coin phrases while holding deathwatch over a continent.

They sat down on the boulder...

After what seemed like countless hours, she said, "I wonder how long we've been here. It feels like years."

He looked at his watch. "I don't know whether we're in time or eternity," he answered simply. "It's nearly four o'clock by this watch."

Through the dense vapor they could see the sun rise, red and sullen, but the mist was so impenetrable that they dared not move around. The day and night passed, almost without their knowledge, and the second morning found them as had the first, by the great boulder. The wind rose with the sun, and when it blew aside the veil of mist, far as the eye could reach, there rolled a sea, white-capped, turbulent, fretful, as if unwilling to leave a single peak to tower above its lordly dominion.

The man and woman followed the collie to the cabin and found some food, then they retraced their way until they could look down over the valley where the town had slept.

Nothing was left. There was not even a prospector's cabin. The shock which had succeeded the first wild dash had been volcanic. And though they called again and again, there came no answer.

"Come on," the man commanded. "Let's go to the Peak. There must be someone there."

They reached the signal station late in the afternoon; no one was there. Looking down from that awful height, they saw on the other side of the range the same desolation, the same watery waste. They seemed to be on an island, alone on a wide, wide sea. Nowhere curled any friendly wreaths of smoke; nowhere was the sound of any human thing.

They went wearily back; there was nowhere else to go. If the gateway had been awful in its solitude, the Peak was still more desolate. There was nothing living there, except themselves, and the dog that followed closely at their heels, making no excursions of its own.

The hour was wearing toward midnight when they sank down by the boulder once more to watch the darkness disappear, and wait for... they did not know what. The man built a huge fire, so that if any other waifs had been left by this wreck of a world they might see the beacon, and perhaps reply in some fashion. They did not talk, except now and then, in a half whisper; they gave monosyllabic queries and replies. The shock that had obliterated a continent seemed to deprive them of all active use of their senses. They moved only in circles, returning always to the place from which they had watched the cataclysm.

It was almost sundown when, with a superhuman effort, they again entered the sunny, beautiful park. The air was balmy, and all remained quite as before. In front of the cabin stood an Alderney cow; as they approached her, she mooed uneasily. The woman looked up, then spoke aloud with the quick sympathy that had always been her greatest attraction. She seemed to understand so readily, whether it was a man's head, a woman's heart, or an animal's wants.

"She needs to be milked," she said, and, pushing open the door, she entered the cabin. There were two rooms, the farther of which was evidently a bedroom. There was a large fireplace at one end of the main room. At one side of it was a primitive dresser, with such utensils and china; on the other were some miner's implements and a shovel. There was a small table and beside it were placed two chairs. There was a rocker by the one window, and a pot of geraniums on the sill; forming a kind of window seat was a long seaman's chest. At the other end of the room stood a desk covered with green oilcloth, and above it was a shelf containing some books and a clock.

The woman took off her hat and jacket and brushed back her hair, then, turning back her sleeves, went outdoors again. Under the rude porch on a slab table stood a number of buckets, and there was a stool by the door. She took a bucket and the stool and walked away a few paces, the Alderney following. As she began milking, she looked over her shoulder at the man watching her and said, "Would you build a fire?"

He gathered some wood and went into the cabin. She threw out the first pint or so of milk, then finished milking and strained the foaming contents of her pail into some crocks left sunning by the door, and went into the house. She found some cornmeal and salt, and deftly mixed the dough, and, arranging the shovel in the hot ashes, set her hoe-cake to bake.

In the meantime, the man had brought water from the brook, and as the woman swung the crane over the blaze, he filled the iron kettle hanging therefrom.

There was some sour milk, and by a mysterious process, she converted it into Dutch cheese. There was some butter and a few eggs, and she found a white cloth and spread the table with the few poor dishes, placing the geranium in the center. As the water steamed and boiled, she caught up a tin canister.

"See," she said with forced gaiety; "let's eat, drink, and be merry, for there's just enough tea in the world for two people to drink once!"

She made the beverage and poured it into the thick cups, and, breaking the yellow pone and piling it on a platter, they sat down to the strangest meal they had ever known.

The man watched her with fascinated eyes. He had never before seen her do anything for herself, yet she presided over the simple meal she had prepared as graciously as over the course dinners of her chef. How did she know how to make hoe-cake?

All through the singular feast, the sparkle and play of her fancy kept them in hysterical laughter. Afterwards, as she cleared away, the same wild mood possessed her. The man wondered if her mind was going with everything else... but as she hung up the towel, her humor changed, and she ran out of the cabin into the dusk as if she could not bear the simple, homely tasks in a homeless world, the firelight and the bounds of a dwelling when Doom was at hand.

The man put a fresh log on the fire and covered the coals with ashes. He would have preferred to remain there, but he knew why she was hurrying back to the mountainside, and he took her coat and followed her.

She was standing by the boulder, looking out over the waters with a despair on her face that made him groan. It was so like what he felt within his own heart. She pointed weakly toward the water, but her lips formed no words.

"No," he answered, "it wasn't a dream..."

Dawn found them still sitting by the boulder. The man shook her.

"Come," he said, "let's go back to the cabin."

"No," she answered. "I can't believe it; we're both mad. We're dreaming the same insane dream! Let's go down, and when we feel the spray on our faces and taste the brine, then it'll be time to believe."

She began the descent with reckless rapidity, and he followed, checking and holding her back. The roar of the surf grew momentarily louder, but though she looked at him with wild, grieving eyes, she went on. A monster wave dashed up over the rocks and wet them to the skin. She flung out her arms and would have fallen headlong into the greedy, crawling water, but he caught her and made his way back. The hot, bitter tears on her face brought her to herself, and with one great sob she broke down, clinging to him and crying until, from sheer exhaustion, she fell asleep.

He carried her back to the cottage and laid her gently on the bed in the tiny room. Her hair was falling about her, and he removed her dusty shoes and covered her as if she were a child. Then he went out into the sunlight and sat down on the doorstep, and tried to grasp the situation.

He had been a very ambitious man, and she had been as ambitious for him as he was for himself; that had been the main bond of union. He was to have made a great place in the world: The applause of listening senates was to have been his; wealth, fame, position... all the possibilities of life were gone; nothing but life itself remained, and barely that. A living might be wrung from nature, but for ambition—what?

Surely somewhere on earth there were other human beings; the destruction, if irreparable, could not be universal. Sooner or later, some hardy sailor would find the surviving peaks of this new Atlantis. At least, if the woman within was not his world, he was thankful that no one else was.

And having looked the grim truth in the face, he, too, slept...

It was long past noon when the dog wakened him, and he started to his feet, determined that, having lost all else, they should keep their sound, clear minds.

He walked about the park, which contained perhaps five hundred acres. There were half a dozen cows, as many horses, some mules, and a few chickens. There was a crude stable and a few farm implements. There was a large tunnel in the mountainside, and some mining machinery lying about its entrance. The dog, seeming to realize some of the responsibilities of life, herded the cattle and drove them toward the cabin.

When they reached it, she was standing in the doorway. She made use of the bathroom, and looked fresh and calm.

"These are our flocks and our herds," he said in greeting. "What should we call them?"

She smiled rather wanly. "Wasn't it Adam who named the animals? You shall have that honor."

"Very well," he answered. "But if this is the Garden, there is an angel with a flaming sword at the gateway. Do not pass it again. Our life is here, here—do you understand? We have to give ourselves time to get used to it, time to realize that we are alive. We must be very patient, because whatever has befallen us, whether we're in the body or out of it, our survival is a miracle, and only time can tell if it is more. Don't look upon the change again... at least not now. You'll stay here, and we'll work together... and be content for awhile."

"Content?" she said. "Content? We will be happy."

II

"Do you remember Gabriel Betteredge?" asked Adam, a day or so later, as he watched her set the house in order after their breakfast. "You know, in times of great mental stress, he always sought comfort and counsel from the pages of 'Robinson Crusoe.' When in doubt, he waited until tomorrow, as Robinson advised; and no matter what his perplexities, he always found just what he wanted in that infallible book. If I remember correctly—it's been years since I read it—Robinson goes on a voyage of discovery the first thing."

"He built a raft to get away from the wreck first, I think," she said reflectively. "Or did he build the raft to get to the wreck? I can't remember. And then he built a house. Somewhere along there, he wrote down his situation in a deadly parallel; I have sometimes wondered if he was the inventor of that style. But he offset the loss of being cast away with gratitude for having escaped with his life. We're not, at least I'm not, sure that belongs on the credit side."

"We don't want to do much exploring yet,"

he answered. "If we have no wreck to supply us with all sorts of things, we have a house ready at hand—not exactly as either of us would have ordered it, I imagine, but better than we could build ourselves. Do you know what all there is in it? We might begin our investigations here."

"'With lamp in hand we will explore,'" she hummed, "but two rooms and a cellar don't promise much. There is nothing to see in this room, except what we see now. And the contents of that chest, which is locked."

Adam tried the lock, then shook the chest. "There's nothing in it, anyhow," he said.

"As to the other room," she went on, "there is a bedroom set—a better one than I would've expected to find in a place like this—and a closet with some clothes in it. The man was about your size, but the feminine garments... well, they are all about the length of my bicycle skirt. And on the shelf is a pile of bedding. There is no trap door leading into either basement or upstairs apartments. In fact, there is nothing else, except a chair. It's very uninteresting."

Adam had been moving about the room, and stopped before the bookshelf. He wound the clock mechanically, and read the titles of the books aloud. A chemistry, a book on electricity, a Bible, a worn copy of Tennyson, the "Yankee at King Arthur's Court," and a patent medicine almanac made up the list.

"There is one mysterious thing," he said, "and that's the packing cases out under the shed. I can't make up my mind what they contain, and I don't quite feel that we ought to open them... but I would like to. They look as if they might hold—"

"Canned goods?" she blurted.

"I was going to say 'books', but I suppose we need canned food more," he assented. "If you're sure they contain oats, peas, beans, or barley, or anything that the farmer knows, that would justify me in opening them." He took up a hatchet, and they went out and inspected the boxes, which were very large and strong.

"Let's not open them just yet," she said. "There is one other treasure in one of the bureau drawers—a box with seeds of almost every kind. They ought to have known most of those things wouldn't grow up this close to timberline."

Adam smirked. "Probably sent by the congressman from this district," he said dryly. "But I'm not so sure they won't grow. Have you noticed how warm it is, how very unlike what it has always been? Let's go to the stables, and see what we can find there."

They went up a path, past a garden, fenced with woven wire, through which the chickens looked longingly. Under some sashes forming a primitive greenhouse, lettuce and radishes were making good headway. Nothing else had come up, though there were many beds, with small slips of board, like miniature tombstones, showing what had been planted. The stables and cowbarn were all under one roof, and would accommodate several horses and a few cows. There was hay and fodder in a lot adjoining, and a few ordinary farm implements, a plow, a harrow, and a cultivator in a shed addition.

"Do you know what it's for?" she asked mischievously, as he pulled out the plow.

"Do you think I've forgotten the farmer vote in my ambitions?" he answered. "I can plow, and I have planted and snapped corn, and cut fodder, and dug potatoes... I wonder if there are any here?"

"Yes," she answered, "in the cellar. At least a bushel, but I forget how thick to cut them. If we were only 'The Swiss Family Robinson,'" she went on, "we'd find yams and pineapples and oranges and sugarcane and bananas coming up between the rocks. As it is, I'm just thankful to the congressman who sent the peas and morning-glories."

"There's only about enough wheat and corn to plant fifteen acres," Adam said, making a rough calculation in his mind. "I'll plow a little over that, so as to have a patch for the potatoes, and get it ready as soon as possible."

"I know how to plant corn and potatoes," she said eagerly. "Just as soon as you get part of the land ready, I'll begin. You didn't know I was brought up on a ranch, did you? I never was very fond of it." She hesitated for a moment, looking reflective once more. "You know, this is all a perpetual round of conditions unlike any theory I've ever heard!" Then she shrugged her shoulders, and stopped at the crude table under the porch to crumb some slices of what looked like a kind of cornbread.

"What is it?" he asked curiously.

"That's to enable us to make light of our troubles," she replied solemnly. "It is, or, at least, I hope it will be, yeast. I found a Twin Brothers yeast cake, and from it, behold the brethren!" She smiled. "I know that raised bread is unhealthy, and that to get the worth of your money you ought to eat the bran also, and that the best bread, from the hygienic standpoint, is made from wheat-paste, and is about the consistency of sole leather... but even if yeast does shorten our lives, I don't know that I'll give it up on that account..."

The planting of their crops took several weeks, and was very hard work, for neither of them was an expert farmer. When the corn and wheat came up, there were almost no weeds, and the quality was better than usual for sod land; but they were kept busy warding off the horses and cattle that preferred the fresh young corn and wheat to the indifferent natural grass.

"I thought," she said wearily, after driving away the intruders for the third time, "that fences were a sign of civilization, but they seem to be the first necessity of the wilderness!"

She was sitting on a rock, fanning her flushed face with her sombrero, when Adam came to her assistance.

"You should've waited," he said. "I was coming, but I had to hitch the team." He turned and looked at her, and laughed boyishly. "The work hasn't hurt you," he said. "You look like a wild rose. I believe I'll call you so! May I? I can't call you by the old name."

She blushed, then turned quite pale, and there was a touch of reserve in her voice as she answered rather too indifferently, "If you choose, I think, oh Adam Crusoe, that 'Friday' or 'Robinson' would be a better name."

"We'll compromise on Robin," he agreed. "'A rose by any other name is just as sweet.'"

"I wish we had a fence," she said, turning the subject hastily.

"We do," he answered. "If we were to

build one ourselves, it would have to be of rocks, but Nature has provided a magnificent stone barrier. We have only to drive the animals we're not using through the gateway, and fasten that little wooden closure after them. There's good pasture outside, and if we need them, we can go after them. Lassie will look after Daisy and Lily, won't you, little dog?" The collie wagged its tail in pleasure. "I'll go and open the gate and drive them through. You help Lassie keep those two back."

She stood uncertainly, and he turned and said gently, "I'll come back without passing through the gateway. I would never pass through it without you. I wouldn't dare." He smiled again to take the edge off. "Now see how nicely Lassie will conduct this roundup."

As he went toward the gateway, her eyes followed him with a look he would hardly have comprehended, it was so full of relief and gratitude. He understood and reassured her without noticing her fears or smiling at her weakness. Every day, and many times, she thanked God that, of all the men who might have been left by this modern flood, it was Adam who had been with her, and was with her in this terrible experience.

III

They had been on the 'island' for nearly four months.

The corn was waving in the soft breeze, and the sun shone bright and hot. Indoors, sweet corn was boiling in the same pot with new potatoes, while in an improvised milk-boiler on coals at one side of the fireplace, peas were simmering. The table was spread, and there was white bread and jersey butter and raspberries. Adam, with Lassie's puppies crawling over him, sat in the doorway and watched Robin put the finishing touches to their Sunday dinner.

His clothing was somewhat picturesque, and he had a tan and thoroughly healthy look. Robin was dressed in an outfit of blue denims. The skirt was rather short, and the top was a blouse, finished at the throat with a broad collar that turned away from a neck still white in spite of much sunlight.

Their months of roughing it had not harmed them, and only the intense sadness in Adam's eyes or the pathetic droop of Robin's mouth, when they thought themselves unobserved, told a story different from that of pastoral content.

Their meal was unusually silent. Sometimes they fell into long lapses of silence; there was so much not to say. In all the past weeks they had worked, almost feverishly, allowing as little time as possible for thought, and never speaking of what was most often in their minds.

Much of the time Adam seemed to be in a dream, only half realizing the flight of time, that made hope more and more hopeless.

Robin said nothing. One would not seek to console the sky with phrases if all the stars were wiped out. She half reproached herself at times for the peace, the something akin to happiness, that had crept into her life. She had long before grown very weary of the world and all it had to offer.

She was stung at the sight of Adam's quiet face, with the repressed suffering that had somehow touched it with a beauty it had not possessed, and she said impetuously, "Let's go out, Adam. Let's go away somewhere, and talk. There's so much I want to ask you, but I haven't dared." He looked up with such a hurt expression that she went on quickly, "Not that; I mean... I couldn't. I've been afraid to put things in words. They grow so much more real then. But now... I'm afraid to keep my thoughts any longer."

They went past the wheat and corn

fields, through a narrow canyon that led them to a valley they had never seen before. It was very beautiful, and the play of the sunlight on the high walls of rock, the murmur of the stream below them, the trembling aspens, the white peaks in the distance, made a scene worthy their attention, but they were blind to it.

They sat down on a broad stone seat. Soon, Adam said, "Now, tell me—tell me how it seems to you."

"No," she answered, "you must tell me. What's happened to us, Adam? Where are we, and why were we left?"

"God knows," he said reverently.

"Do you think it possible..." she asked slowly, "... that we are dead?"

"Oh, I don't know!" he broke out, with a return to something of his old childlike impatience. "Sometimes I think it's all a dream, and soon I'll wake up and find myself in my dingy old law office. But you... you aren't a dream. These mountains aren't a dream. Lassie barking down below there isn't a dream; and these callouses on my hands are real enough in all conscience, and no dream could last so long. Sometimes I think we have been hypnotized and carried off and left on an island somewhere. Sometimes—do you remember the man who computed the vast number of 'mysterious disappearances,' and formed a theory that the earth was being sorted out before the opening of the last vial, or some such stuff?　Do you think we can simply be another disappearance?"

"I don't know," she said.　"It seems easier to believe that, easier to believe anything than that the whole world has disappeared."

"Then I think sometimes," he went on, "that there are evil powers—I know this sounds as if I had lost my mind, and maybe I have, I'm not sure of anything—but it seems as if there might be an explanation if we believed in geniuses who have power over us.　Maybe you and I, who so often found fault with the poor old earth, are being punished by banishment from it? Maybe we're being prepared for some great work?　I don't have very much religion... and yet I suppose I do believe in a divine purpose behind things, a directing power that wastes nothing.　I've tried to think of why this thing should come upon us, you and me, of all the world; and while it seems like an evil thing, a terrible and overwhelming disaster... when I realize that it might have befallen just me, alone... then just the fact that you are here makes it seem almost good.　Do you understand?"

"Yes," she said quickly.　"I've felt the same way.　When, at first, I felt as if I should curse God and die, I only had to remember you to fall upon my knees for thankfulness. Even if a dozen other people had been left instead, no one would have understood as you have. Oh, I would infinitely rather be alone with you than in the utter loneliness of the company of a lot of men and women who would drive me mad with their complaints and inefficiency. I don't know whether it's a dream, or heaven or hell, or the work of some black magic; I only know that, if it is a punishment, it has been commuted because you share it. And yet how selfish that sounds, as selfish as love itself. I ought to wish you were in a better, happier place, where you could carry out your ambitions—" She stopped, and her eyes filled.

"Don't worry," he said grimly. "If that is selfishness, I'm selfish to the core. I've gone over the whole list, and I don't know anyone I would rather sacrifice to companionship with me in this exile than you. My parents were old; they could never have borne the shock. My sisters would be unhappy without their own families. None of my women friends could have met the exigencies of such an existence as you have. And as for men, by this point we would all have been barbarians together. You have kept me sane and alive."

"But are we sane?" she asked. "I think I could stand it if I only knew we were sane and alive. It's the feeling that I don't know anything, that this valley, these mountains, may fade like the baseless fabric of a dream. And sometimes I think that it may be real, all real except for you, and that I'll find myself here all alone, dead or alive, sane or mad." She shuddered. "God! How horrible it is!"

"That thought has never troubled me," he said. "Whatever has put us in this dream together will keep us together to the end. You haven't wanted me to go far away from you, so we've worked together; I've even let you do work that was unfit for you, because I knew you would prefer it. You were more frank about it, but you didn't feel any more strongly than I did. I couldn't, I can't bear to have you out of my sight."

"Have you ever thought that it may be real?" she asked hesitatingly.

"What? That it isn't a dream, and that we are sane and alive? Yes, I have thought of that, too. If it's real, how universal is the destruction? We know now, pretty well, from the time that has passed—by the way, how long is it?" He stopped with a sudden dazed look, and turned to her.

"It was the first of May," she said softly. "Now it's nearly the end of August."

"Four months!" he said in shock. "I didn't realize it; I must've been more stunned than I thought. In that case, it seems as if there can't be anything left of this continent, except detached peaks here and there, where other mountain ranges have been. There may be other men and women waiting as we wait for a sail, a sign, a message, and they don't know any more than we do when it might come. The alteration in the climate has convinced me that the waters on our West are those of the Pacific; it's been so warm and pleasant. I've tried to imagine what kind of a winter we may expect, or will the winter of our discontent be made glorious summer—"

"By three crops of strawberries, like California?" she interrupted.

"Maybe," he said, smiling. "As for the East, that may be the Atlantic, or the Gulf; it seems more probable that it's the latter. The St. Lawrence district was said to be the oldest section of this continent, and it's reasonable to suppose the earth's crust was thickest there, and along the mountain ranges. I suppose the continent has gone to make another layer, a stratum, on top of the pliocene, and after a while the waters will subside, or some volcanic action will raise up a new continent. If there are any ships anywhere, on any seas, they'll search every degree of latitude and longitude. Our flag floats, did float, all over this globe; if it still flies anywhere, we'll see it again."

"If I did," she said irreverently, "I would feel sure we were in heaven. It was beautiful before, but what wouldn't it mean now, Adam? But do you have anyone left on earth; if this continent is all gone, who would look for you? I had relatives, or I did, but they didn't even know of my existence."

"There's not a soul," he answered. "In this country, it would've been one chance in ten million. You might've done it," he said, half jestingly, "but you're here."

"Yes," she echoed, "I'm here. Adam, how long will it be before you're satisfied that no one is left, no one in the sense of any civilized people, with a country and means of circumnavigation?"

"A year," he answered, "perhaps more, but at least a year, anyhow. I won't give up hope until then."

IV

The corn hardened and the wheat ripened, and was harvested in truly primeval fashion. Adam cut the wheat with a scythe and Robin followed him, binding it as best she could. They shocked it together, and then began hauling it to the barn with the horses and bob-sleds, their only vehicle. The stacking was weary work and progressed slowly. Adam watched his co-worker toil over the sheaves, and then took them from her and pitched them on the stack haphazard.

"You shouldn't bother with it anymore," he said, "not even if we live on hominy all winter. Have you ever been in Mexico? Well, Hawaii was called 'the land of poco tempo,' but Mexico had the right idea — there isn't any work there for the work's sake. I mean there wasn't, and we can take a lesson from them. We don't need to hurry; the legislature won't meet this winter, and there'll be no grand opera before spring. Daisy and Lily will do our work for us. We'll find a bit of hard, smooth ground, and then we won't muzzle the cows that tread out the grain."

"Willingly," gasped Robin in pleased

agreement, climbing down from her slippery eminence on top of the load of grain. "But do you think we're going to have any winter?"

"That is one of the preeminent things that no one can predict," he answered. "In a dream, you're likely to have any kind of weather... and on a submerged planet, we have no precedents at hand to tell us what to expect. By replanting the vegetables right along we've had a consistent crop. As long as we have this kind of weather, things will grow, and I suppose we better let them. Shut in as we are, it doesn't seem likely that any very fearsome winds are apt to trouble us; and if there is a wet season, on this slope we'll have good drainage. If the worst comes to the worst, there's always the tunnel. Could you make that cheerful and homelike?"

Robin smiled rather sadly. "It'll do to put the grain in," she said, and they walked on silently.

The spot they finally selected for the threshing floor was brushed as clean as twig brooms would make it, and the wheat was spread out upon it. Adam and Lassie drove the cows over it leisurely, and between times Adam experimented on a thresh. When he finally had one that served the purpose—and found he could use it without fracturing his skull—the cows were released, and he went on with the work. Seated on a boulder close by, her sombrero tipped well over her eyes, Robin fanned the grain, and converted it into a coarse cracked wheat with a venerable coffee-mill.

"I'll make you a Mexican mill when I get through with this," said Adam, "but you can't use it, because it's too hard work; I'll have to be the miller. It's a rather simple affair, and dates from before the days of Noah. It's made with two stones—preferably sandstone—the lower of which is hollowed out bowl-fashion, with a hole in the center; the upper stone is rounded, and fits in the bowl, and has a hole in it about four inches from the edge, in which a stout wooden handle is inserted to turn it. The two stones are ground together until they become smooth. Then they're placed on four other stones as rests, and a blanket or cloth is spread underneath to catch the meal. The grain is poured around the edge of the upper stone, and works down. It makes a pretty tolerable flour."

"How handy you are!" she said. "Isn't it a good thing we hadn't civilized the whole world to such a degree that only patent high-grade flour was used? Where would we be now without the simple devices of the good people of the Stone Age, and their decendents on whom we looked down with so much scorn?"

The snapping of the corn was an easier matter, and it was piled in the tunnel until they were ready to shell it. Then Adam did what he called his "fall plowing," and left the bare brown sod to lie fallow.

So far as possible, they had retained the manners and customs of the world that had left them. There was a tolerable supply of clothing, and a good deal more household linen than could have been expected. Robin concluded that the owners of the cabin had not been married long, and the bride—knowing what kind of a place she was coming to—had thought more of her house than of herself. All the feminine garments had to be re-fashioned. Robin made her skirts short enough for mountain climbing, and, dreading the time when her one pair of shoes gave out, she wore sandals fashioned from yucca leaves by Adam's clever fingers. As the hair-pins lost themselves, she braided her hair in a long tail, the curling end of which fell far below her waist.

The little house was kept neat and clean, as if it were headquarters for all the labor-saving inventions in the world, and their meals were as well served as if a corps of servants had been in attendance. They were simple, and often a little monotonous, as meals must be where there is nothing except what grows on one's own plantation. They had no tea, coffee, sugar, spices, or foreign fruits. However, the hardship of manual labor and plain food would cure most cases of indigestion, and they didn't suffer.

One day early in December, Robin woke to the sound of a steady drip, drip of rain, accompanied by an indescribably mournful wind. In the other room, she heard Adam piling on the logs, and shivered.

Perhaps the winter had come after all.

It had been hard enough when there was plenty of work, and the free outdoor life; if they should become prisoners, how would they, how would he endure it? She dressed quickly, and met his cheery "good morning" in kind, and over their breakfast they discussed the possibility of this storm being the first of many. They decided that they must get the corn into such shape that the tunnel would be available for the hapless cattle, or even for themselves, if need be.

"We'll go up there and shell corn all day," said Adam. "It isn't really cold, and you can wrap up a bit. I wish I'd thought to take a lot of stone into the tunnel to build a bin at the end to put the corn in. I don't know how we'll manage it."

She disappeared into the bedroom and came back presently with a few grain sacks. When Adam opened the door, he was nearly ready to abandon his plan.

"You'll be wet through and through," he said. "I can't let you go."

"Then you can't go, either," she answered.

"But I have to," he said. She was standing by him, hardly reaching his shoulder, the sacks over her head. Catching her up in his arms, he banged the door behind them, and ran up the slope to the tunnel, where he deposited her laughing and shaking the water from her curly hair.

As he had said, it wasn't cold, and they sat down near the mouth of the tunnel, turned the tops of their sacks back over corncobs, and shelled the corn in silence. At last a little sigh from Robin made Adam look up quickly. Her hands were bleeding.

"Robin," he cried angrily, "how can you be so cruel! I don't want you to do this work; there's no need. I forgot to watch you. Besides, I know you're tired. You didn't sleep last night; I heard you moving around."

"Then you didn't sleep, either," she responded quickly.

He flushed through the tan, and scooping some dry leaves together into a bed, took off his coat and folded it for a pillow.

"Lie down and rest a little now," he said, "while I go down to the house and see what I can find for lunch. Then you can have a good sleep this afternoon."

He was gone several minutes, and when he came back with some sandwiches in a tin bucket and a dozen scarlet radishes dripping in his hand, he stopped, appalled.

Robin was at the extreme end of the tunnel, sitting on the ground, laughing and crying and talking extravagant nonsense.

Had she really gone mad, at last? Adam put down the bucket, and walked toward her unsteadily.

She didn't stir, but went on chattering in the same absurd way until she saw him; then she cried excitedly, "Oh, look! It's kittens, real little tame kittens, though their mother won't come near me yet. She's over in that corner."

Adam saw her green eyes, and though distrustful, she wasn't entirely unfriendly. Emptying the bucket, he ran down to the sheds, and came back with some milk, which he poured into the top of the pail and set down before the kittens. They lapped it eagerly, and as the two human beings withdrew discreetly, the cat crept out of her corner and joined in the feast. When it was over, Robin took possession of one tiny ball of fur, and Adam of another, while they made their own meal. Then Robin curled up among the dead leaves and slept like a child.

It was growing dusk when Adam awoke from his daydreams. The tunnel looked like a small grain elevator. On one side Robin still slept, but the old cat was nestled contentedly at her feet, and the kittens were playing sleepily over her.

"What is she dreaming?" Adam asked wearily, aloud. "All day, I've sat here and dreamed dreams that can never come true. I know it; I feel it. I told her a year... but I am as sure now as I shall be in six years, that there is no hope. The watch-fire is out tonight—the first night in eight months. I'll relight it for her sake; not that she's any more deceived than I am, but she'll be happier to believe that I'm still hopeful. What will be the end of it all? How can it end?"

"The same old way," came her sleepy voice from the leaves, "with the 'got married and lived happily ever after' formula."

She sat up and rubbed her eyes, and stretched lazily, to the discomfort of the kittens, who retreated hastily. As she struggled to her feet and a knowledge of her surroundings, her face changed pitifully, and she sat down again and cried miserably.

"Oh, it was so real!" she sobbed. "I can still see it now. We were back in the old house—in the library, do you remember it?—and Walter was at the piano, and Louis had just asked me how to finish his last story. Did I answer out loud? Oh, which is the dream, for that was as real as this!"

Adam stood and watched her. He heard the beating, steady patter of the rain and the lowing of the cows, and there was not even a star in heaven to look at him from its accustomed place with a friendly, twinkling promise for the future. There was nothing left. So far as he was concerned, the earth was without form and void. There was nothing to wait or hope for. There was nothing to live for, neither cheerful yesterdays nor confident tomorrows.

What was the use in living?

He looked down at the slender creature lying outstretched almost at his feet, shaken with the agony of long-repressed grief, and then at his long, muscular hands.

How little it would take to end it all for both of them!

A mist came over his eyes and he stooped, his hands outstretched toward her white throat. They fell on the rounded curve of her shoulder. He stopped the caress as he stopped the other impulse, and shook her instead.

"Let's go home," he said.

They went into the storm.

V

The next morning dawned clear and warm, and Adam, coming in with his milk-pails, held out his hand to Robin. There were three ripe strawberries.

"See," he said, "they're the harbingers of spring, or a California climate, and either way makes our gain. California, without fogs and fleas, is heavenly enough for most people."

Nevertheless, they completed the shelling of the corn, and made a bin for it at the end of the tunnel, removing the cat family to the house, where Lassie viewed their arrival with jealous eyes. One day, when they had been hulling corn for nearly a week, Adam sat down and began laughing. "Do you know how much corn it takes to plant an acre?" he asked.

"No," said Robin, blankly. "I know something about the number of kernels to the hill—'one for the cutworm, and one for the crow, and one for something-or-other else, I forget what, and one to grow.' Why?"

"It takes eight quarts to plant an acre. We've raised about thirty bushels to the acre, which is very well for sod. That'll make over fifteen thousand pounds of meal and hominy, and will feed us for seven years, even if we eat six pounds daily." He chortled. "Unless there's a winter season, when we must do something for the animals, there's not the slightest use in planting more than an acre. As to the wheat... even with a light yield, there would be fifteen hundred pounds to the acre. We'll have fresh vegetables all the time, and there'll be any quantity of potatoes and cabbage and beans."

"And yet people starved everywhere, and it seemed to me that the farmers were the worst off of all."

"They farmed to make money, not to live, and they had no control over the markets. They had to sell or build barns—it's only Dives who can afford to tear down the old ones and build greater. It was easier for them to sell cheap to a man who took their wheat and held it until it could be sold back to them as dear flour. They were eaten up with mortgages and pests and interest. Have you noticed that there are almost no insects here, not even flies and mosquitoes? They were never so bad in the mountains, but apparently they've been wiped out with the rest."

"Tell me the truth, Adam," she said suddenly, "speaking just of the physical part of it... would you regret this year?"

He stood up and stretched out his arms,

a splendid type of manhood, smooth-shaven, with clear-cut features, bronzed, square-shouldered, and powerful.

"Oh, you're magnificent!" she cried involuntarily. "It's done you good, great good. You're twice the man you were in strength and health and resource; and if only we'd been cast away on an island, knowing we were sure to be rescued some day soon, I wouldn't be sorry at all."

He blushed and answered frankly, "Without the mental strain, I wouldn't regret this year. Sometimes, when I'm sure it's a dream and that soon we'll wake up, I can't help wondering whether we won't wish we had fretted less and enjoyed it more. When I come to think of it, I believe it's the first time since I was a child that ways and means have not troubled me. It was a good thing to work as we have, to keep our minds employed, but now that we're sure that starvation is five or six years away, we might as well drop the old, headlong rush to get more than we need. That's been the trouble ever since men began to make history. It was the same thing—power, conquest, riches, everything; too much to eat, too much to drink, too much to wear—"

"Well, you can't say that of us," said Robin ruefully, looking down at her made-over gown.

"Well, maybe not, and I don't mean that

there was ever a time when there was a general excess, but I mean that was the tendency. There would've been plenty for all, if part had not taken more than their share; as for the other part who had not enough, they only longed for the opportunity to simulate their unwise betters. When they could, they took too much, too, if it was only to drink and forget their misery. We could've lived so well and so easily, if we'd lived more simply, coming more directly in contact with Nature, as you and I have this year."

She shook her head doubtfully. "This hasn't been real life at all. We've only kept alive. We haven't read anything or done anything or helped anyone—"

"Except each other and the animals dependent on us. On the whole, I believe that we have accomplished about as much as when we were devoting most of our attention to paying board-and-rent bills. We've helped each other more than we can measure. We would've died, had we been left alone with our thoughts. All of life is not in cities, nor even in books."

She did not answer for some moments, and then said slowly, "If it were a dream, and we were going back to the old life, what would you regret most?"

"If we were going back to the world we know, I'd regret a good many things. First, I suppose, that I didn't realize sooner that we must be going back, instead of letting myself be utterly overwhelmed. Second, I'd regret that we haven't kept a record of our lives from day to day. There's other writing I'd want to do, but there's no paper, and I don't know how to make any."

"There's still plenty of time to do all that," she said. "What else would you wish you had done?"

He looked at her, for there was something in her voice he did not understand, but her eyes were turned from him. "I'd regret that we hadn't talked more. Do you realize we've been very silent? And we used to have so many things to talk about in the old days. I'd have twinges of remorse that I didn't make more of your companionship when I had it, instead of raising more corn than we can eat in half a dozen years, and letting you tear your hands shelling it." He stooped and kissed one of her slender hands.

She withdrew it quickly; there had never been even a touch of the sentimental between them.

"What would you regret?" he asked suddenly.

She shrank a little, and her eyes looked far away, past the gateway. "Some of the things you mention; very much that I hadn't encouraged you more to go on with your work, but mainly..."

"Well... 'mainly?'"

She jumped down from the rock where she had been sitting, and answered evasively, "I don't think there is any 'mainly,' unless it's that when I had such a good chance to be a hermit, I couldn't remember all those wonderful Mahatma practices that make one so good and so wise. The only formulas I've really tried hard to recall are for cooking without sugar, or spice, or fruit."

VI

It was Christmas Eve, and the night—being in a reminiscent mood—was chillier than usual. Adam piled up the logs until the whole room was full of the warm glow. "Let's hang up our stockings," he said, with an attempt at gaiety.

Robin spread out her hands with a gesture of comic distress. "If only I had a pair to hang!" she said. "But they gave boxes in England, didn't they? I noticed the other day that the rain seemed to have come through the shed roof, and I'm afraid the contents of those packing cases may be the worse for it, especially if they happen to be sugar. Do you think it would do to make ourselves presents of them? If you do, please give me the smaller box; I'm sure it has hairpins and needles and darning-cotton in it."

Adam laughed. "We'll give them to each other," he said, "and maybe you'll find some stockings in your box, if there's no box in your stockings. We can dream of their contents all night, and—who knows?—we may have a merry Christmas after all."

Robin hardly knew the place next morning. Adam had risen early and decked every available spot with kinnikinnick until the room fairly glistened. "I wish I knew how to thank him," she said.

"Do you like it?" he asked as he came in. "I was afraid I'd wake you while putting it up."

"Like it!" she answered. "Why, Adam, it's beautiful. You're just an ideal Santa Claus."

When they had finished their breakfast, they went out and looked at the boxes.

"You open yours first," she said; "it's so big I know it doesn't contain anything nice, so we'd better save mine until the last, and then I can divide it with you. What do you think it is? You have three guesses."

"It might be a piano from its size," he ventured.

"No," she said decidedly. "It's not the right shape."

"Or maybe it's a featherbed; I don't know of anything I want less."

"It's too large for that; now guess, really."

"As a matter of fact, I expect it's mining machinery, which will be about as much use as another chimney. But here goes nothing!" He brought his hatchet down vigorously between the boards at one end, where a slight crevice promised some leeway.

"Oh, be careful," she cried "even if there's nothing in it but stove-polish and wood shavings, the nails and the boards are absolute treasures!"

He proceeded more gently. There was plenty of hoop-iron, which he removed carefully, and the nails were withdrawn with as much caution as if they had been someone's teeth, considering there were no more on earth to draw.

When the top of the box was finally off, and a quantity of papers removed, they gave a simultaneous cry of delight.

The box was full of books.

They took them out, one at a time, with little exclamations of pleasure as an old friend came to light. Sitting down on the ground, they piled the books around them on the papers, and, opening favorites here and there, read to each other and themselves until long after noon. It was really a fine library, well chosen, covering a wide range of subjects and including an encyclopedia and an unusually fine edition of Shakespeare.

"Isn't it the most beautiful Christmas present you can imagine, Adam?" she asked. "If you aren't satisfied with this, it must be because, in the old slang, you 'want the earth!'"

"But we haven't even opened your box," he said.

"I don't want to," she answered slowly.

"Somehow I feel as if we'd better stop now and leave well enough alone.　Let's enjoy this awhile.　The other box might spoil this one, or at least the day."

Adam laughed with good-natured tolerance.　"How absurd!" he said.　"Let's see what's in there.　You know you said yours would be the nicest; besides, if it contains sawdust and last year's almanacs, I'll have to divide it with you, and we may quarrel over the Shakespeare."

He opened the box while she stood watching him with a strange unwillingness. It had been labeled, "This Side Up," and on the very top there was a wooden case.　He put it in Robin's arms, and she opened it with trembling fingers.

She replaced the broken strings, adjusted the bridge, tucked the violin under her chin, tuned it... and straightway escaped from every sorry care of earth.

Adam went on unpacking the box.　It mainly contained materials for writing—all the paraphernalia that a fastidious student required.　There were many notebooks and, at the bottom, a large, handsomely inlaid writing-desk.　The name on the cover made him start, then call her.

She put down the violin reluctantly, and then stooped and kissed the vibrating wood with sudden feeling.

"It's a Steiner," she said.　"You know the story of Steiner's violins, don't you?

No? Some day, maybe, I'll tell you. Can you open the desk?"

He found the key and unlocked it. There were some letters, a few papers and memoranda, and a journal. Adam turned to the last page written, and read:

"'Have just completed arrangements for transportation of my effects to the mountains. Close study of various phenomena convinces me that I may have been in error, and that the cataclysm is much closer at hand than I have thought. Within a few months, I'll burn this book, and confess that I should be written down an ass, or turn to it to prove myself a prophet. From the lofty nest I have chosen, I expect to be able to write the story of the coming flood. It'll be of great value to posterity to have a calm, scientific account, quite free from any tinge of superstition or religion. I have today written my Boston skeptics, forwarding copies of my calculations, with references to former inundations, and reasons for believing the Rocky Mountain region the safest at this time. All geologists agree that—"

Here the journal terminated abruptly.

Robin hardly seemed to comprehend its full significance; or possibly she just was not surprised. She touched the book as gently as if it were the napkin over the face of the dead.

"It's not to the wise that God has revealed himself," she said softly. "Where is the hand that wrote this? You must finish it, Adam. Here are the blank pages waiting for such a chapter as was never written on earth."

But Adam only looked at the half-written page unseeingly. "It's all true, then," he muttered to himself; "it's all true."

He walked away with a painful precision of motion, almost as if he were drunk; he neither heard nor saw anything, yet was conscious of everything, and while he thought he had been hopeless before, he knew now that he had never given up hope, never until that moment ceased to expect a rescue.

Robin took her violin and went indoors. Presently, he heard its liquid notes stealing out to him, like a power unknown and divine, brushing its fingers across his heart, the harp of a thousand strings.

She played for a long time, and when she ceased, in some strange way, he found that he was comforted.

VII

They had been sitting by the fire in silence for a long time. Robin had been sewing, but the blaze had sunk too low to see by it, and her hands were folded idly upon her mending. She put it aside and went to the window. It was a very dark night, and the stars shone brilliantly. The stars had come to mean a great deal to them both, although neither had ever said so.

Only the stars remained unchanged. "The thoughts of God in the heavens" were the same, whatever might be His thought on earth.

She sighed so heavily that Adam asked quickly, "What is it?"

She answered with a nervous laugh, "I was thinking of the old legend, that the souls on other planets call ours 'the sorrowful world.' What made it so sorrowful, Adam?"

He thought for a moment. Then he answered, "Ignorance would cover it all. But to be specific, intemperance, sensuality, avarice, and poverty. I don't mean drunkenness only, when I say 'intemperance.' I've known a few tea-toddlers in my time who were as intemperate in their eating as any one could be in the matter of drink. I think intemperance in its widest sense was the great curse of our time, anyway; drink and tobacco and tea and coffee; and as to our eating, there was too much, of almost everything on earth that was not food, but which could be over-salted and over-peppered, and treated with tabasco sauce. We overstimulated every activity of the body, and spent our lives doing all kinds of things in which there was no sense. Think of reading one or two morning and evening papers every day. To be sure, we said there was nothing in them, but we used up our eyesight over them, and let a stream of silliness and scandal dribble through our minds. As to the things we wore—"

Robin laughed. "I know," she said. "The sewing-machine didn't save work; it only made ruffles. A dressmaker once said to me, 'It's a good thing for me that these women haven't sense enough to spend their time and money on themselves, in making their bodies free and strong and beautiful. But no; they would rather have a stylish dress than a graceful body. They don't care to be beautiful themselves; all they want is a pretty gown to cover their ugliness.' Isn't it strange that we never seemed able to realize that the Greek fashions were immortal because they were beautiful?"

"Still, I don't think the fashion of the Greek women would be very convenient for housework," ventured Adam.

Robin shook her head. "You only say that because some woman has said it to you. The Diana of the Stag wore the first rainy-day gown. The Greek dress was capable of so many modifications. If I were making a handbook of proverbs for women, I should say, 'A good complexion is preferable to any fine dresses, and glossy and abundant hair defies any wrath.' I believe in the simplification of life. I understand just how Thoreau felt when he threw out that knickknack because it had to be dusted daily. There are very few things beautiful enough to be worth that amount of trouble. But maybe that's because I don't care for knickknacks, and I loathe dusting."

"You ought to have been Japanese," said Adam. "There was one in college, in my class, and one day when I was fretting over something I couldn't afford he said, in that immensely polite way of theirs, 'You I cannot understand. It's so with all Americans; whatever you have, you more would get of, and wherever you are, you would go from. You're only happy when you get something, and never that you are yourself.'"

"I wish," said Robin, "we knew how to make paper; of all the fascinating things in Bellamy's 'Equality,' there was nothing I liked so well as the idea of paper garments, to be burned when one got through with them. Think of never having any washing and ironing, and always having new clothes!"

"I wonder whether we could invent some of those things over again," said Adam, reflectively.

"I couldn't spare you any of my precious rags, if you could," said Robin.

"Most of the paper was made out of wood, anyhow," answered Adam, "and the ash trees that grow here in any quantity were considered particularly fine for that purpose."

"'God made man upright, but he hath sought out many inventions,'" quoted Robin, "and now we're going to seek them over again. I can't imagine how anyone could ever make a typewriter, but the type-and-hand-press are easy enough, and if you can make paper, we may yet live to read our 'published works.' You probably don't know that I used to have a skill for dropping into poetry."

"Did you? That's another of the things you never told me; but speaking of Thoreau," answered Adam, "I recall what he said of the amount of work necessary to sustain life beside Walden Pond. It took six weeks out of the year, and that was in a most forbidding country. In such a valley as this, two months ought to be sufficient to more than feed and clothe us; but then, he didn't have to make his own clothing."

"And out of nothing particular," interrupted Robin.

Adam laughed and went on. "Did you ever hear of a man called Hertzka? He was an eminent Austrian sociologist, and he figured that if five million men worked a little less than an hour and three quarters per day, they could produce all the necessities of life for the twenty-two million people of Austria. By working another two hours and twelve minutes daily for two months, they could have all the luxuries also. And not just for a few—not for the Court and the nobility—but for all. There could've been music and pictures and books and theaters, and sufficient food and clothing. Isn't it strange that when we might have been so happy, we preferred to be so wretched? For even if we had all we wanted ourselves, we couldn't escape the sights and sounds that told of abject misery."

"It was always so," Robin answered moodily. "We always had the poor with us. History always repeated itself."

"Still, it didn't exactly repeat itself," Adam said. "Our dark age would've done for a golden age in the past. Greece was glorious for a little while, but her literature tells us of her ideals. The isles of Greece, where Byron contracted his last illness, would've left him to die among the rocks twenty-five hundred years earlier, because he had a lame foot. We, at least, were kinder to animals, and that means a great deal."

"I don't know. Maybe. It seems to me I've read of a hospital for sick animals on the island of Ceylon a long sometime B. C. Lady Mary Wortley Montagu—or was it Lady Hester Stanhope?—said she'd traveled all over the world, and had only found two kinds of people—men and women. I fancy the same thing is true of all the ages, as well as all the countries."

"No," Adam said, shaking his head, "our ideals change. The scheme of life laid down by Christ was foolishness to the Greeks and a stumbling-block to the Jews, and there were still plenty of Greeks and Jews in our day—by 'Greeks' I mean people whose ideals were purely intellectual, and by 'Jews' those who saw no good except a material good, no God but the God of Mammon. They wouldn't hear either Moses or the prophets, and the statute of limitations was as near as they could come to the Sabbatic year. The Greek and the Jew have stood ready with their cup of hemlock, their crown of thorns, for every Christ-spirit that has ever come to earth. Yet more people read Socrates, and believed in the Nazarene every year. I don't mean in the church; the workingman didn't go to church, but he uncovered his head at the name of Christ, the first lawgiver who confounded the scribes and Pharisees, and ate with publicans and sinners."

"But Moses was the first lawgiver to forbid taking the nether millstone as a pledge," objected Robin.

"True," he admitted, "and the laws of Moses would've made the world over. He was the greatest writer on political economy this earth's ever seen. His absolute fiat against the alienation of the land would've done more for the common people than all Adam Smith's theories of free competition and Fourier's dream of a perfected communism. But who would've known of Moses, except for Christ? The Old Testament would've been merely the sacred book of the Hebrews and, except as a literary and historic work, of very uncertain historic value. It would've been unread, as the Koran and other books of a similar nature were unread."

"And yet you don't believe in the divinity of Christ," she said slowly.

"No," he answered. "But is that necessary before one can believe in his teachings? The truth is always divine. What difference does it make whether the one who utters it is human or divine, bond or slave? The truth remains the same. A fable is only another name of a parable.

We have the story of the lost sheep—that's a parable—and that of the lamb that muddied the stream—that's a fable. One is sacred, the other profane, but both are fables, both parables. When you take them away from the context, it's as easy to feel for the lamb eaten by the wolf as for the one that was rescued, and has been immortalized in picture and song."

"You're probably right," she said. "I never thought of it in just that way before."

And saying goodnight, she went to her room.

Adam thought he heard her humming, "Away on the mountains cold and bare."

VIII

The discovery of the incomplete journal made a subtle change in Adam. He had been silent and self-absorbed from the first, but he had never quite given up hope. Even now, Robin sought to keep up the pretense, and, dreading the despair which she saw creeping over Adam, she began to artfully seek some means of interesting him in something else. The question of a proper place for the books gave her an opportunity, and Adam suggested that he build an addition to the house.

They planned it as eagerly as if it were to be a castle, and spent days looking for adobe, but finally decided that logs would be better, and Adam's ax could have been heard ringing from morning until night.

A log house was not exactly a work of art, but it required no little skill to build one, and took a good deal of time when the logs for the floor had to be planed and squared to make a matched board floor. Sometimes Robin went with Adam, and worked or read; sometimes she took him his luncheon at noon, because the trees were a fair distance from the house. The logs had to be "snaked" across the rough ground and down the mountain, and when the floor had been laid and the location of the window decided upon, Robin planted morning-glory seeds where it was to be.

After much pushing and hauling, the logs were finally put in place, and the roof battened down. The window was truly worthy of a medieval castle, for it was simply an oblong hole, boxed in with a casement made from some scraps of boards, while a slab shutter, swung on leather hinges, shut out the elements.

The chinking was a simple matter, and when it was all done, including a doorway into the main room, Robin was unfeignedly delighted. They made rows of shelves with the packing cases and arranged the books. It was not an extensive library, but it occupied one side of the room, and was a godsend to them.

Under the window Robin placed the green covered desk, and placed on it Adam's writing materials. Along the inside wall, Adam built a bunk, after the fashion in miners' cabins, and with a mattress stuffed with the soft inner cornhusk, a pillow from the other room, and blankets from the one tiny closet, the couch looked sufficiently inviting.

On the floor, Robin spread mats made from plaited cornhusk, and in the doorway hung a portiere, woven from the same material on a loom that a Navajo might not have utterly despised.

Adam's scanty wardrobe was transferred to pegs in one corner of the room, one or two stools were set first here, then there, until Robin was sure the best effect had been secured, and when all was done that they could accomplish with the means at hand, and the morning-glory blossoms came peeping in at the window, the room was by no means unattractive.

Then Robin's housewifely soul took refuge in housecleaning, and she scrubbed and arranged and rearranged, while Adam repaired or invented furniture, until inside and out their little domain was as perfect as they could make it.

Between them had again fallen one of those long silences they dreaded, but seemed powerless to prevent. As the voice of the turtledove was lifted in the plaintive notes of nesting time, Adam harrowed three acres of the plowed land and planted it in wheat and corn. The perennial garden was flourishing, and there was nothing to do. Adam said so one day, with an air of calm finality.

Robin regarded him uneasily. The time had not yet come when he could sit down and write, though she had brewed an excellent ink, and the paper waited on the desk in his room. She considered for a moment, then said brightly, "Don't you remember what Myron used to say? How when his friends got rich, they first built a beautiful house, and then went abroad for three years? Let us go traveling; wouldn't you like it?"

The briskness with which he acquiesced proved how well he liked it, and he started out at once to get the burros and make ready for the expedition.

Robin baked and prepared as well as she could.

"It's a good thing I had a Southern grandmother," she proclaimed as she put her beaten biscuit in the Dutch oven and pulled the coals over it. "And it's a good thing my mother crossed the plains and learned how to make biscuit in the mouth of her flour sack, and," as she rolled out some crackers, "it's a blessed good thing I went to cooking-school. But I wish that, instead of being so particular about the knobs on the candlesticks, the Pentateuch had given Sarah's recipe for making cakes with honey. Not that I have any honey, but I am sure we'll find some on this trip."

When they were all ready and the burros stood waiting at the door, with Lassie jumping wildly about them, Adam wrote a placard which he stuck in the framework of the door. The stock had been turned loose on the mountainside, and the house and stables secured as well as possible against any storms that might arise. The kittens had possession of one of the sheds. The puppies were to accompany them.

Robin had put on her long unused shoes,

and a new gown that she had made out of a dark blue serge found hanging in her room. Adam looked at her approvingly from under his wide sombrero. She turned back, after going a few paces, and read the card.

WAIT!

APRIL 5th.

Back in two weeks.

Look for smoke.

As she passed into the canyon that hid their home from sight, Adam saw her brush her hand across her eyes.

IX

They traveled due west, crossing the two ranges, wending their way through dim defiles and along steep canyons, until they saw the sea. Here its mood was summer-like. Even in the short time that had elapsed, it had worn itself a broad, smooth beach, and wide tracts of land between the sand and the base of the mountains proved that the earth had been thrown up, or that the water had receded. They had not looked upon the ocean for many months.

They picketed the burros on the rank, salt grass and built their campfire early, and while Robin set the potatoes baking and began her supper preparations, Adam went scouting along the coast. In less than half an hour he came back with a quantity of clams, which he threw down before her as proudly as if they had been foreign battle-flags. She gave a little feminine shriek of delight.

"Now I know why we brought that inconvenient iron pot," she said. "Bring it here, please."

Adam brought it, and watched her slice up onions and potatoes and stir in the various ingredients.

"It's going to be the best chowder you ever tasted," she said, "even if we don't have any bacon. When you write the tale of our adventures, Adam, don't put in how many things we ate."

"They might think it's a voracious tale if I did," he answered, dropping some more butter into his mealy potato. "Do you remember how the Swiss Family were always worrying for fear they wouldn't have enough to eat?"

"Yes, and how they went out and killed an elephant for breakfast, and a herd of wild pigs for dinner, and had a buffalo apiece for supper. And don't you remember how, when the boa constrictor killed one of their zebras, little Fritz asked pathetically if boas were good to eat?"

They laughed over their supper and then, having made sure that they were out of reach of the tide and the fire would keep, and the rifle was close at Adam's elbow, they spread their blankets and said "goodnight." It had been an exciting day.

It was past midnight and the moon was waning when Adam was wakened by Lassie's cold muzzle against his face. He sat up and called to Robin.

There was no answer, and her blankets lay tossed on the other side of the fire.

He started up and listened. At first he heard only the sound of the sea; then there came, mingled with it, the clear notes of her glorious voice. Holding Lassie in check, he went down to the beach.

Robin stood well out on the shimmering sand, the waves lapping softly almost at her feet, and he heard the plaintive music, and caught the words—

"Oh, for the wings, for the wings of a dove,

Far away, far away, would I fly, and be, and be at rest."

Her voice quivered when she came to the words, "In the wilderness build me a nest," but she sang on, and Adam recalled the words of hymn after hymn, anthem after anthem, for she sang nothing else. He heard the bitter cry of the De Profundis, Handel's triumphant "I know that my Redeemer liveth," and then she began, "He watching over Israel slumbers not nor sleeps."

His eyes filled, and he saw the tents of his regiment. She had written by every mail, and across her letters, at the top or bottom, she had put those five bars from "Elijah." Though he did not believe it, for he didn't have the early Hebrew ability to see Israel in his own race, and the to-be-spoiled Philistine in every Filipino, it had comforted him in that sickening campaign—surely, surely if he, an American "non-com," had spared a Filipino now and then, He watching over Israel had not been less merciful.

Her voice died away; it was the first

time she had sung that year, though she was
a very perfectly trained musician. Indeed,
in the old days, Adam had first sought her
acquaintance because of her music.

Adam returned to the camp; he knew
instinctively that she preferred to keep
this to herself. He was lying quite still
when she came back, and controlled every
muscle when she bent over him. She
regarded him intently for a moment, then
went to her blankets with a heavy sigh that
Adam knew was for him. She had sung out
her own sorrows.

Their nighttime vigils seemed to do them
both good, for they shook off their
melancholy tendencies, and before the end
of the first week, their tour was beginning
to be thoroughly enjoyable. They did not
find cocoanuts and bananas, but they did
find plenty of strawberries, and long,
prickly vines that would be covered with
raspberries, and wild grapes and choke-
cherries and currants, which they planned
to transplant, for though the Western coast
was more beautiful and in some respects
more convenient than their hedged-in
valley, they preferred the valley.

Already it had come to mean home.

They traveled about fifty miles
southward to the end of the island, making
desultory trips up into the mountains to
see if anywhere, on land or sea, there was
a friendly wreath of smoke, and every night
their watch-fire glowed from the highest

peak in their vicinity. The island narrowed to a single range, detached peaks rising here and there from the sea. As they rounded the southernmost point, Adam said, "We ought to name it; that remarkable Swiss family always named places."

Robin looked at the bare, stone walls rising sheer above the waves three hundred feet, and her lip curled.

"Let's call it the Cape of Good Hope," she said.

"In the name of wonder, why?" asked Adam.

And she answered, "Because we are past it," and then would have given anything to have recalled the bitter words.

The Eastern coast was wilder and more picturesque, but the traveling was correspondingly slower. Something in the formation of the coast caused a terrific surf, and at many places there was scarcely any beach, and they found themselves compelled to climb along trails that made even the burros dizzy.

When they had been gone ten days, Robin said, "I'm beginning to feel like a grandmother—no, I don't mean that I feel so old, but that I'm beginning to long to see the chicken and cat-children, and the new calf, and... and everything."

Adam laughed, "I've been thinking we ought to hurry; that place of ours is growing so entrancingly lovely in memory that, last night, I dreamed that I dwelled in marble halls!"

However, they were destined not to reach home without at least one adventure.

A day or so later, as they toiled up a painfully steep ascent, Lassie sounded the note of alarm and, catching up the rifle, Adam ran ahead. As he rounded a point in the rocks, he came upon a Rocky Mountain goat engaged in combat with a cinnamon bear. The bear was hardly more than a cub, and was carrying off one of the goat's young kids. The goat, horns down, was fighting viciously, though weak from loss of blood.

It would be interesting to know what one wild animal thinks when another wild animal, from its point of view, comes to the rescue. Adam carried a lasso over one arm. In an instant, it flew through the air, dropping over the brown bear's shoulders.

The bear released the kid and tumbled backward over the cliff, as much with surprise as by the force of the jerk on the rope, taking that treasured item with him.

It took some time to capture the wounded animals, bind up their hurts, and get them down the pathway leading to the beach. For down there was a beach, the best one they had found on the Eastern coast, and as they put the goat and her kids down in the grass, Adam said tentatively, "If you aren't afraid, I can go home and get the horses and the sleds. It isn't a great way, and I believe I can be back in three hours—I'm sure I can if the beach goes as close to our park as I think."

Robin acquiesced, and as soon as he was gone, she began gathering driftwood. When she had quite a little heap, she made a fire with the coals they carried in the pot. It is doubtlessly more romanticist to build a fire by striking flint rocks together, but a pot of coals had its uses in a matchless universe. Then she found a long, stout club and put one end in the fire, where it smouldered sullenly.

"There now," she said conclusively, "if my bear acquaintance calls, I'll present him with 'the red flower.' I didn't learn the 'Jungle Books' by heart for nothing."

Meanwhile, Adam was striding over the beach at a rate that brought him to the little cove and the high wall of rocks that shut them in on the south in a little over an hour. Two of the pups had gone with him, and they raced on ahead as he came in sight of the house. Everything seemed to have an air of welcome, and the horses whinnied joyfully when he called them from the gateway.

The pathetic placard was still there, and he crumpled it in his hand, and went in and opened the windows. He milked one of the cows, and, gathering some green stuff in the garden, started back with the team and the sleds. Once down the steep decline and over the rocks at the south, they went on rapidly.

Although he had wasted no time, it was past one o'clock when he saw her familiar figure a great distance off. She hurried to meet him. They had not been separated for so long all that year, and realized the unconscious strain in the sudden detachment. They said nothing of this, however, though they clasped hands for a moment. Then Robin spoke to the horses and stroked their necks as they bent their heads and rubbed against her affectionately.

She had spread their table on a broad, flat rock, but before they had their own meal, she warmed some of the milk, and they gave the kids their first lesson in drinking out of a bucket. Afterward, it took just a few moments to strike camp. The burros were already packed, and the goat with her kids, all hobbled, were placed in the sled, and the cavalcade started on its way.

X

"Do you know, Adam," said Robin, when they had walked a mile in silence, "do you know that you are a bit of a fraud?"

"Well, yes," he responded, "but I didn't know you knew it. Is the discovery recent?"

"Never mind about dates, but tell me why you didn't use the rifle instead of the lasso? What did you even take it for?"

"I took it for your peace of mind. I didn't use it for several good and substantial and sentimental reasons. This last year, I've grown to understand your horror of killing things. We've done very well without sacrificing any of our dependents; in fact, it would seem like murder to slaughter those animals around us. And it's such a little world, it seems a pity to kill off any of its inhabitants. To tell the truth, I hope the bear got away all right. This is maudlin, I know, but I don't want my hand to bring the first death on all there is left of earth. Incidentally—there's no ammunition."

He stopped the horses, while Robin readjusted the kids to make them more comfortable and took the lame one in her arms, then they moved on.

Presently, she said, "I am so grateful for these kids!" There was so much enthusiasm in her voice that Adam laughed and asked why, and she answered, "Like you, I have both sound and sentimental reasons. The sound one is that we'll need their fleece unless—why, goodness gracious, Adam, there's a baking-powder can of flax in the dresser, and I never thought until this moment that we can plant it."

"True," answered Adam, "but given flax or fleece, what would you do with it?"

"Spin it," she answered pithily. "Of course you think I can't, but it happens that I once lived, when I was a little girl, very near to an old woman. I don't refer to her age, but her ideas. She carded and spun and wove and dyed all the family clothing. She made her own soap and wouldn't have a stove in the house. She had eight children, too, and all of them turned out badly. I used to go there off and on; I think she looked on me as a kind of sinful amusement. Anyhow, she told me the world was going to ruin, and those women were poor creatures who couldn't spin a hank of yarn, or gin a pound of cotton, or heel a sock. She shook her head over me when she found I couldn't knit, but she set a garter for me at once, and during the seven or eight years that I went by her door on my way to school, she taught me all those marvelous accomplishments." She sighed. "I daresay I've mostly forgotten them."

"What are the sentimental reasons?" asked Adam.

She looked at the kid as it nestled against her shoulder.

"I have a fancy," she said, "that Nannette and her children are going to minister to a morbid mind, and help pluck a rooted sorrow from the brain. The world was getting too healthy. Has it ever struck you that neither of us have been sick for a day this year? I've had to mother the chickens, but there's been no suffering. I'm not glad to have pain come into the world, but it's good to be able to alleviate it. We'll put Nannette in a sling till her leg has a chance to set, and by the time it's well, she won't want to leave us. As for the kids, I expect they'll be like the plague of frogs, and we'll find them in our beds and our ovens and our kneading troughs. Oh, Adam, there's the house! Doesn't it look dear and homey?"

She put the kid back on the sled and ran on, pointing out this and that, the growth of the corn, the afternoon radiance, until they reached their doorway.

Then there were a thousand things to do.

First Nannette was made comfortable in the stable; then the chickens were summoned to a meal of yellow corn, and when Lassie drove the cows into the barnyard, each was congratulated in turn upon her calf, and those interesting, if wobbly, bovine infants were carefully inspected.

After supper, they sat down before the fire, very tired, but the nearest to happy they had been in a year. The dogs were lying about them, and the thump, thump of first one tail and then another told the story of canine content, while the kittens walked over them impartially.

"What a strange thing human nature is!" Adam said. "The only thing needed to make our life perfect is that it won't last. The moment, if that moment ever comes, when it's real no more, it'll become ideal."

"I know," she said dreamily. "Things in the world used to be too good to be true. This must stop, if they're to be good at all."

XI

"It's the first of May," said Adam. "It is a year ago today. Should we pass the gateway?"

"Not now," answered Robin. "Wait until afternoon. I'm so busy this morning."

She was sitting at the table teaching half a dozen little chickens to appreciate hard-boiled egg. The wounded kid was lying in her lap, one arm was about it, and an adventurous kitten looked over her shoulder. As she tapped on the board with one slender forefinger, the chickens, hearing their mother's bill, began picking up the fragments of egg. She had rounded out wonderfully in a year, and Adam realized for the first time that she was a very beautiful woman.

"Suppose," she went on, "you begin your book today. Write your description of a year ago. It'll never be so clear again. There's plenty of time before we go. Besides, if it's a dream, we'll want the written record to show what dreams may come."

Adam hesitated a moment, then went to his desk. She had spoken truthfully—the events of that day would never again be so clear—and as he began to record them, they marshaled themselves before him until he found himself writing with a dramatic power that fascinated and amazed him.

It must have been some time afterward that Robin sneaked in and set a glass of milk, some biscuits, and strawberries down on the desk beside him and then went out, taking the dogs with her. He did not notice another sound until she called him to supper.

While he did the evening work, Robin dressed herself in the garments she had worn the year before. As soon as she could make others she had put them aside, awaiting the awakening or the rescue.

The heavy cloth skirt and the silk waist were put on with a strange reluctance. Years ago, the old doctor in "The Guardian Angel" said our fine china became our tombstones, but surely our garments may become the graveyards of our emotions, and hold sharp or sweet remembrances long after they are past wearing. In spite of some tan, Robin found the face that looked back at her from her mirror infinitely more attractive than it had been the year before.

Adam started a little when he saw her. Then he drew her hand through his arm, and they went to the gateway.

As he opened the gate, she turned and looked back. The sun was behind the mountains, and the shadows were long and dark. They heard the sounds of the various creatures settling into quiet for the night, and Adam sent back all the dogs but Lassie. They went slowly and wistfully. Robin stooped and kissed Prince on his white forehead. As Adam closed the gate, she said half fearfully, "Will we ever see them again?"

But he did not answer. He took her hand and led her to the boulder.

As far as the eye could reach, they saw what they expected to see.

Half a mile away, the sea rolled in on a tolerably level beach; here it thundered and roared against a sheer cliff. Among the rocks, they could see the nests of many wild-fowl, and gulls flew by them.

They sat down on the rock and waited until midnight. Then they went home.

The dogs received them boisterously, and the kid bleated faintly from its corner. Robin bent over it anxiously, then warmed some milk and fed it. When Adam came in with some fresh water, she was swinging slowly to and fro in the rocker, singing softly an absurd nursery song:

"Sleep, baby, sleep. The stars they are the sheep; The big moon is the shepherdess; The little stars are the lambs, I guess. Sleep, baby, sleep."

"It needed to be cuddled," she said in as matter-of-fact a voice as if all lambs were sung to sleep regularly. "You know,

dear old Professor Carter said there would
have been no wild animals if we hadn't made
them so; but now, if you're willing, you can
put her with Nannie."

When he came back, she had gone into her
room.   There was nothing more for either of
them to say.   There was nothing to do,
except to hope for a sail, since they no
longer hoped for an awakening.

XII

The work on the book progressed rather slowly. Adam often had to refer to Robin when his memory was at fault. At first she had gone away, to leave him alone with his work, but as he referred to her more frequently, she sat with him, sewing while he wrote, a frame of morning-glories behind her, or reading with the keen enjoyment of one who renews a pleasure long foregone. When he seemed to be going along smoothly, she sometimes stole away and gave herself up to long hours with her violin.

One afternoon, she tapped on his casement. His work was lagging, and he rose gladly and went out with her. They walked up the path and through the gateway to their boulder, and sat down.

"Talk to me," said Adam.

She shook her head. "About what, most worshipful lord? For I am but a worm of the dust before thee, and all my tales are of the homely tasks of baking and brewing. Naught is there worthy to be set down in thy book." Then, with a sudden change of manner, "Oh, Adam, there are eighteen new chickens today! The Plymouth Rock hen stole a nest, and they came off this morning. And there is some news, too. The flax is in bloom. It's so pretty."

"When do you expect to weave your first linen?" asked Adam.

"Oh, I don't know, but it's good to know there'll be some to weave. Do you remember Andersen's story of the flax? I was thinking of it this morning as I pulled out some weeds, and how when it was pulled up and cut and hackled, it said: 'One cannot always have good times. One must make one's experience, and so one comes to know something;' and when it's woven and cut up and made into garments, it still says, 'If I have suffered something, I have been made into something. I am happiest of all. That is a real blessing. Now I shall be of some use in the world, and that is right, that is a true pleasure.'"

"If one only knew he was to be of some use," Adam said wearily, "if we could see the justification of our suffering."

"Then we should be as gods," answered Robin. "I like the song of the flax, 'content, content;' and when the linen is worn out, it's again tortured and beaten until it becomes paper whereon an eternal word is written. I used to wonder why Andersen was given to children; not that I wouldn't have them read him, but he's one of the profound thinkers of the world. No one had 'Andersen clubs,' or professed to find deep and wonderful esoteric truths in his stories, but they're there. Do you remember my girls' club down on—I don't think there were any streets, but the inhabitants called the place 'Kerry Patch'?"

"Why, no," said Adam, "I didn't know you had one; why didn't you tell me?"

"That was ever so long ago, ages and ages—when you came to see—" She paused a little, and then spoke the personal pronoun that tells the whole story, for a woman can say "him" in such a way as to betray unspeakable heights of adoration or abysses of loathing. She went on slowly. "You weren't one of my friends then; how could you be, if there existed anything in common between you two? That sounds dreadful, but you know all about it so well that trickery is useless."

"To tell the truth, I never cared anything about him at all," Adam answered quickly. "Like a good many others, I was enthusiastic over your voice. He asked me to the house to hear you sing, and I went, and was glad of the chance. And you've never sung for me once this year."

"You never asked me," she answered. "'A mute priest loses his benefice.' But I was speaking of my club. We studied Andersen all winter, and got more out of him than a lot of us who pored over Ibsen. Andersen has a more beautiful, a more inspiring philosophy. Every nation has its story of Psyche, the lost soul of things, but none

is more beautiful than the tale of Gerda
and Kay. There were children in that club
who were cruel, horribly cruel, and one day
when we gave an entertainment for them, one
of the older girls recited the story of 'The
Daisy and the Lark.' They cried as I'd
cried over it years before."

"I remember," he said. "It broke my
heart when I was a little shaver. I
couldn't give such a sad story to a child."

"Oh, yes, you could," she said, "if the
child needed it. The world was cruel,
Adam, cruel; I used to wonder sometimes why
God didn't blot it all out before, as He has
blotted it out now. Once in another club,
a big, swell affair, there was a Humane
Society program. One woman, in a Persian
lamb jacket, spoke on the evils of the
overcheck; you know how they get that wool?
And women nodded, the feathers in their
bonnets torn from the old birds, while the
little ones starved to death, to show their
approval, and clapped their hands gloved in
the skins of kids, sewed in cloth soon
after their birth so they couldn't grow a
fleece, and tortured all their short lives,
and went home to eat pate-de-foie gras and
broil live lobsters, thanking God they
weren't like the rest of men, if only they
let out their horse saddles a hole or so.
It was horrible—the cruelties men
practiced to gratify appetite, and that
women were guilty of for vanity. I suppose

I'm a monomaniac on the subject, but to me, we never seemed far removed from barbarians, when we went clothed in the skins of wild animals and decorated with their heads and tails and feathers, like so many Sioux chiefs. The varnish of civilization isn't dry on us yet. Why, if a ship should come here now, do you know what they would do first? They'd say they wanted some fresh meat, and offer to buy Lily, the fattest of the cows. If we wouldn't sell her, they'd probably take her anyway."

"Kill Lily," cried Adam, angrily. "They'd have to kill me first; nothing on this place is going to be slaughtered while I can protect it." He went on more slowly, a little ashamed of his heat, "I feel a sense of kinship with all these creatures that would make it impossible to kill them. It's like the woman whose Newfoundland dog died, and a friend asked if she was going to have him stuffed. 'Stuffed!' she said; 'I'd as soon think of stuffing my husband!'"

Robin laughed and, leaning over, tweaked Lassie's ear. "If we're to be stuffed, we prefer to have it an antemortem performance, don't we, little dog?"

The sun dropped behind the tall peaks, but its dying light still covered sea and shore. They rose as if for the benediction, and looked out at the waters before them...

Then, stunned, they looked at each other

and grew white to the lips, and Robin knelt down and flinging her arms around Lassie sobbed and laughed.

Adam never took his eyes from the coming ship.

XIII

The ship bore steadily toward them, but night was coming on so rapidly that her lines were obscured. They could not even tell whether it was a sailing vessel or propelled by steam.

"There's one thing for certain," said Adam, excitedly, "it's coming this way, but very slowly. I suppose that's to be expected of a ship sailing unknown waters. They have nothing to go by—they only know, of course, what part of the round globe they're on."

She answered almost apathetically, as if she found it difficult to talk, "It seems as if good sailors would lay anchor at night, when they don't know their course and there's land in sight—land that's never been explored."

"It does seem strange she should come right on," he assented. "For surely no ship has ever sailed these seas before. Perhaps..."

"Perhaps what?"

"Perhaps she's been clear around; maybe this is the only bit of land left above a world ocean."

Robin shivered a little, and Adam turned toward the beacon that had glowed in vain for a year. It had been built on a high, altar-shaped rock across the gorge, where it could be kept up without leaving the park. Robin went with him, and they gathered a pile of timber that insured the brilliancy of their signal until morning. Adam piled on the logs until the blaze leaped far up in the darkness; then they went back to the boulder and sat down to think and wait.

"See how the wind's rising," said Robin, breaking a silence of an hour, during which even Lassie had been motionless.

"But it's toward land," answered Adam.

"But the same wind that brings us the ship may dash it to pieces on this awful coast."

"True, but she's far enough out to make herself secure. Oh, Robin, suppose she sails around us and goes on!"

"That's impossible," answered Robin. "The people on that ship are as anxious to find us as we've been to see them, if they're civilized at all."

Adam crossed the gorge and added fuel to the fire. For a time, the wind increased in velocity until a stiff gale was blowing, then, as the small hours came on, it waned, and the beacon flared straight up once more.

"I wonder where's she from?" said Adam.

"I wonder where she is now."

"I feel sure," he said, "when morning comes, we'll see her riding the waves out there. And think of it, Robin, we can go!"

Robin made no reply, and her very silence made Adam repeat, but as a self-addressed question, "Go where? Yes," he went on quickly, "go where, Robin. Suppose the ship's all right, and that she stops, and the crew aren't pirates and are willing to take us aboard... where are we to go? Is there any place on earth that can mean as much to us as this island? Suppose Asia, or Africa, or Europe are still in existence, we wouldn't regain our friends and relatives, and life would be harder with strange people, under a strange government, far more so than we've found it here, even without so many of its luxuries."

Robin shook her head sadly. "At first, Adam. Then we'd learn their language and their customs. New friends are speedily acquired, and as for relatives—well, in the scheme of life, relatives don't count for much. There always comes a time when they step out of our lives, anyway."

"But as to happiness?"

Her face paled a little. "Have you been happy here?" she asked, without raising her eyes to his, and then went on, not waiting for a reply, "If you have been, it's been in the care of our little family of dependents, who don't need you half so much as the great family of human dependents. Rest assured, if there's a continent over there across the darkness, it's peopled with beings who need the devoted and unselfish labors of such a man as you. You'd find your work easily enough—the work you've been saved for, the work you must do."

"But if there's no continent left?" he queried.

"In that case, there must be islands; there were many mountains higher than these, and they're peopled, no doubt. Should we not go to these other orphans, deserted by Mother Earth, our brothers and sisters, through our common calamity?"

Both were silent, engrossed in their own thoughts. A return to the world meant going back to the uncivilized rush of civilization. It meant the eternal question of what shall we eat, and what shall we drink, and wherewithal shall we be clothed? It meant the old competition, the stern old law of the survival of the brawniest. Above all, to Robin, it meant separation from Adam, for once more in Rome, the customs of Rome must be followed.

To do Adam justice, this was a contingency which did not enter his mind. As he had said before, whatever had put them in this dream together would keep them there, so that when he thought of relinquishing all the comfort and ease and quiet of his present life, all the loving animals, the cosy little house, the tiny fields, the blooming garden, it never occurred to him that he must relinquish more than all these things, more than the peace and harmony, that which, unconsciously, had come to be the very guiding star of his life.

"I wonder if whoever is left cares for grand opera?" said Robin, rather grimly.

"Why?" asked Adam in so startled a voice that she laughed hysterically.

"It's the only thing I know well enough to make a living at it," she said laconically. "I think the fire needs some more wood, Adam."

As he replenished it, her words burned themselves upon his brain, and he realized in an instant that a return to the old world meant giving up this supreme friend, all that he had left in the world, all there was for him in any world.

Impossible.

He turned to go back to her, some kind of a hotheaded vow on his lips, but she had left the boulder and walked down almost to the edge of a precipitous cliff which they had called "Lover's Leap" in jest. She stood there quietly, watching the gray dawn, and his heart impelled him to go to her and take her in his arms. As his love revealed itself to him in all its power, it seemed impossible that he should know it now for the first time.

Why, why, had he been so blind? If the ship took them away—!

He walked unsteadily down to her, resolved to say nothing. If she wanted to go, her wish should be sufficient.

The dawn came slowly, but it came at last. As the darkness lifted, a slight fog settled over the face of the waters. Instinctively, they recalled that other night when they had watched through the mist and his hand closed over hers. The sun was well up before the east wind dissipated it and left only the dancing waves, brilliantly blue, stretching away into the dawn. On all that broad expanse, there was not so much as a cockleshell vessel afloat.

Robin turned and looked to right and left in bewilderment, and then at Adam.

His chest was heaving, and as his eyes searched her face he cried, "Thank God," and gathered her up in his arms.

She nestled there without a word.

They crossed the gorge and scattered the brands of their watch-fire, and walked on down to the cove.

Suddenly, Lassie came bounding toward them uttering short, excited barks. They quickened their pace, and as they came in sight of the beach discovered the object of her alarm. Against a small promontory, lying on one side, was the ship they had sighted the evening before. It was a hopeless wreck, and had borne to them no living thing.

Yet it had served its purpose. It had revealed their love for each other, and told them that they had hoped against a second deluge in vain.

XIV

As Adam went about his morning's work, he was filled with a sense of gladness, an exaltation of life he had never known before. He stretched out his arms, as if to let all the glory of the earth meet the profounder splendor of his soul. As he walked down the garden path he looked with affection at the flowers they had planted together. But for the absurdity of it, he could have woven a wreath of them and worn it. But the world had reached that height of civilization where the symbol of the glad and living thing was too emotional; always and everywhere, we preferred the dead thing, the skin of the seal, the shroud of the silkworm, the straw that was left after the flowers were gone; and Adam was still civilized.

He accepted his happiness without a question. It was too real, too keen, too great a revelation for him to stop to analyze it. He knew it in every pulsation of his heart, in every imagination of his mind, and with the quickened senses of the lover, he perceived that Robin's feelings differed from his own. For a year he had been lost in introspection; now they seemed

to have changed places, and she grew silent
and almost reserved.

"What is it, dear?" he asked. "No, don't
try to evade an answer. We mustn't stop
being frank with each other now."

She did not reply at once, and when she
did her voice was so low that he had to
stoop to catch the words. "Do you think
you love me as fully as you might have
loved someone else, younger and happier
than I, better fitted to you? It doesn't
seem as if you could; you never did in the
old days, you never even thought of it."

Adam laughed lightly. "I beg you to
spare me, for this isn't 'so sudden' at
all." Then seeing that her mood forbade
teasing, he went on seriously. "Really, I
mean it. It's true, I never made you pretty
speeches in the old days, nor stopped to
consider whether I might have done so had
things been different; but then, I never
made pretty speeches to anyone. From the
very beginning, I've taken you as a matter
of course. It always seemed as if we'd
known each other from the very first. You
entered into my plans as if you'd known
them, as you might if we'd gone to the same
little red schoolhouse. I wish we had! I'm
jealous of the years when I didn't know
you."

"But a whole year," she said doubtfully.
"Are you sure it isn't just loneliness and

proximity?"

Adam kissed her fingers one at a time. "You're going to beg my pardon for that someday," he said. "You're not at all vain, my sweetheart; how could I help loving you?"

"That's just what I'm finding fault with," she said with a sudden twinkle of fun in her eyes. "You've managed to keep from it so long. But seriously, I'm not the kind of a woman I imagined you'd care for. I am—at least, I was—very weary of life; I knew too much about it. And I'm older than you."

He looked at her critically. "You were, a year ago," he answered. "I don't know how much, two or three years—"

"Five," she said.

"Well, five; but this last year, you've been growing younger. The very fact that you were tired of the old life made it less of a strain for you to give it up. The tired look is all gone, even from your eyes, whereas lots of gray has come into my hair. You'd learned to live in yourself and your music. My whole scheme of life was wrapped up in the social existence of our time. In a way, I lost more than you did. I've learned a good deal this past year. Five years ago, if I'd loved you, there would have been many inequalities between us that don't exist today. Now it seems to me we are as absolutely mated, as much parts of one whole as the two halves of the brain, or the right and left ventricles of our hearts. It's no disparagement of you or of myself to say that no boy could appreciate you. The measure of a man's manhood is his ability to understand the highest type of womanhood. As to your being worldly, that's all nonsense." He stroked her hair a few minutes in silence, and then said, half quizzically, "You might question me, if I said it, but this is what Balzac said of women like you: 'A woman who has received a man's education possesses a faculty which is the most fertile in happiness for herself and her husband; but that woman is as rare as happiness itself.'"

She looked pleased, but she didn't reply, and he went on.

"Do you still doubt me? Well then, know that I've loved you from the very beginning, for love, when it comes, is a retroactive law of our being. If I'd loved you less, if you'd seemed less a part of me, I might've realized it sooner."

She shook her head. "I've known that I loved you for a long time. Months," she said.

"Then you ought to have known that I loved you," he answered quickly. "Don't you think it's possible to love with our souls, our subconsciousness, and only realize with our slow brains—after months, or even years—what our hearts knew at once? Even love has become more or less of a mental process. We reason about things instead of feeling them, and yet when we come to our last analyses we don't know anything... we simply feel. When the scientist says, 'The amoeba moves out of the shade into the sunlight because it wants the sunlight,' he bases his postulate upon what he feels, and believes that the atom feels. This's all that he knows. We don't seek warmth because we've calculated its effects upon us, but because we feel cold. Oh, we've starved our feelings to feed our brains, until the mind believes it's the immortal part of us, instead of realizing that what we 'know,' we are merely rediscovering, while what we feel is our conscious perception of the infinite. If we had the courage to be true to our feelings instead of our thoughts, I believe it'd be a better, and certainly a truer, world."

"Do you really think more people are guided by thought than by feeling?" she asked with a good deal of surprise.

"Maybe not in one sense," he answered. "A great many people are carried along by their impulses, their transitory emotions, which are not, properly speaking, 'feelings' at all. They make what someone calls the 'fatal error of mistaking the eddy for the current.' But among educated people, it seems to me that we think too much, especially of our own thoughts, and feel too little. All this year, I haven't said that I loved you; I don't know if I've thought it, but I have felt and lived it. Sometimes I haven't been thoughtful—"

"You've always been too thoughtful," she interrupted.

"No, but when I've been inconsiderate, it was because you were myself, the best self that we overlook sometimes, but return to with unfailing loyalty. You weren't bone of my bone and flesh of my flesh; that's a very low and material view of what you've been and are to me, heart of my heart and soul of my soul. I can't think of a life apart from you, for you are my life. Marriage is not a matter of a license and a ceremony and Mendelssohn and gaping crowds and a tour. We don't need anyone to tell us that what God has joined cannot be broken apart by man. All this year has been a long wedding of every thought and feeling and desire, until I've looked into your eyes to see my own wish. We've thought and thought, but that way lies madness. Now I feel that all the world we've lost lives for us in every glorious possibility in each other. For I know that you love me."

"Yes," she said, "I think I've loved you all along, but it never entered my dreams that you could love me. Even now, when you tell me, it doesn't seem as if it could be real, either by the mental process or by that of feeling."

He caught her in his arms and kissed her, a kiss so long and tender that it left her clinging to him, breathless and half awakened.

"Don't think," he said, "feel—feel my heart and know that every beat is for you, that every atom of me calls for you, and every drop of blood obeys, as it would command you. I've tried to reach the ideal of the love that says, not 'thou must be mine,' but 'I must be thine,' but I've failed if you can still doubt me."

She flung her arms around his neck with sudden passion.

"This is the greatest, the most perfect dream of all," she said. "I think it must be heaven."

"A new heaven and a new earth," he answered gently.

XV

The derelict did not afford them much amusement or information. The waves soon beat her to pieces on the savage rocks. Apparently, she had been a ship plying between Western ports, probably San Francisco and Honolulu. In the washed up wreckage were a few pounds of rice and some brooms of what they believed to be sugarcane. Nothing else.

"Not even a lemon!" Robin said grimly. "Think of living all one's natural life not only ten, but ten thousand miles from a lemon."

Adam laughed sympathetically. "It's like a yachting party I remember—we found that the boat we'd engaged had been taken by somebody else, and our group had to be divided. Later in the evening, we discovered that we had all the sugar and the other crowd all the lemons. ''Twas ever thus from childhood's hour, I've seen my fondest hopes decay: I never wanted something sour, but what molasses came my way.' Never mind, dear. We'll go and plant our sugar, and by the time it's ready to sweeten anything, a whole cargo of lemons may have floated into harbor right at our door."

They crossed the ranges to the western coast where there was lower ground, better fitted to the supposed requirements of rice and cane, and had a good deal of amusement out of their ignorance, neither of them having more than a misty idea about either rice or sugar before they reached the stage to be served together.

It was quite late when they finished and camped for supper. Remembering their trip of a few weeks previous, which now seemed so long ago, Adam said, "Are you too tired to sing, dear? It's been so long since I've heard you."

She stood up and thought for a moment, and then, putting back her loosened hair, began with Bourdillon's "The night has a thousand eyes," and sang on and on. At last, turning to Adam with a little fond gesture, she altered the words slightly and sang:

"Like a laverlock in the lift, sing, O bonny bride! All the world was Adam once, with Eve by his side. What's the world, my lad, my love? What can it do? I am thine, and thou art mine; life is sweet and new.
If the world has missed the mark, let it stand by, For we two have gotten leave, and once more we'll try."

"'Once more,'" Adam repeated. "Once more, my darling! Oh, life is sweet and new for us; we can afford to lose the world! When will you come to me, love, when?"

She shook her head with a little wilful laugh, and all the glistening glory of her hair fell about her like a wedding veil.

"Wait," she said, "wait a little. The flax is not nearly ready for spinning yet; can a bride forget her wedding dress? Besides, how can we be—" she paused, and let her silence fill the gap, "when I know neither of us knows any ceremony more dignified than hopping over a broomstick?"

They started homeward, walking slowly through the dimly lit mountain gorges, talking the ineffable nonsense that lovers never weary of. As they came to a brook that rushed noisily down the ravine, Adam stepped across, and held out his hand to her.

"Wait a moment," he said, "just where you are, dear, and say this with me: 'Over running water: my love I give to you, my life I pledge to you, my heart I take not back from you while this water runs. Over running water: every seventh year, at this time of the year, at this hour of the night, I will meet you here to renew my betrothal; death alone to relieve me of this vow.'"

"Is that all?" she asked wonderingly. "Over running water, while this water runs, while there is any snow in the mountains, or rivers upon land, or waters in the seas, or clouds in the skies, when the world is old, and the sun burned out, and time grows weary, I shall love you still, always and forever. What is it all about, love?"

He clasped her close, and did not answer at once. "Don't you know that old Irish betrothal," he said, "which would've been enough, even in that hard, unromantic world of ours, to have made you legally my wife, if said over any Scottish stream? I thought you knew; you're sure I wouldn't trick you? You know I couldn't?" He put her head back and looked into her shining eyes. It seemed to him he couldn't bear even a look of reproach.

She raised her hands, almost as if she were placing an invisible crown upon his head, and let her arms fall about his shoulders.

"Then I am your wife while living water runs?"

"Forever and forever," he replied.

"Oh, wait, wait just a little," she answered.

XVI

Adam found a note beside his plate in the morning.

"I will be back before five o'clock," it said. "I must think."

He didn't sit down to the table she had spread for him, but called the dogs—Prince was missing, and this was a relief to him. Nothing could happen to her when Prince was with her.

His first impulse was to follow her, but he resisted it, and he, too, sat down to think. Lassie whined uneasily, and he stroked her head absentmindedly, and finally went out and tried to work. The hours dragged away, and by four o'clock he could stand it no longer. He went to the gateway.

As he unfastened it, he saw her coming toward him, but she stopped and he joined her, and together they turned back to the boulder. He noticed that she was very white, and that her eyes looked as if she hadn't slept, but he only said, "Have you thought?"

"Yes," she answered, "I've thought."

"And decided?"

"No," she said wearily, "we have to

decide together. We aren't children, Adam, nor are we in any way the prototypes of those first parents of ours, Adam and Eve. I think sometimes that, ever since their day, their children have been walking in a blind circle, eating not the fruit of knowledge, but of the knowledge of good and evil. And what do we know, you and I, after all these years? Are you sure what we ought to do? It's as if God had taken us into a conspiracy to renew the old—or create a new—scheme of existence. Maybe we're being tried, tested, to prove whether or not we've learned our lesson. We must be brave enough to think, not what is our will, but what is our duty. Think of the awful responsibility, whichever way we choose."

"I can't," said Adam. "I can't think of anything but you."

"I feel the same," she said, moving away, "when you hold me close. But we must think."

"I have," answered Adam, gravely. "All my life, I've thought. I've wanted the perfect companionship of the one woman in all the world who could give it; I've always known she would come. I've wanted a home; I've wanted to see my sons and daughters grow up around me. I wanted to be a power for good in this world of which we are a part, and where we live for some good purpose, if there is any purpose in life.

I've conducted myself so that I can look a good woman in the face and offer her my life, for whatever it's worth, without damning recollections to come between us. My children will have a clean heritage of blood and name. The family tree was scoffed at in America, but, thank God, mine was an oak that had weathered many storms. Not very great folk, but honest, upright, fearless men and women, true to their king or their country and their faiths; true to their ideals, too. Any man who gives his children such a heritage can say with more truth than Napoleon said to his soldiers, 'Fifty centuries look down upon you.' I wanted to make the world a little better for my life, and I wanted my children brought up to feel that their lives belonged first to their country, to live or die for her."

"I know," said Robin, softly. "I used to think I'd drape the flag over my baby's cradle, and embroider it on his pinning blanket."

"We're probably a pair of sentimental fools," he went on, "but I believe in sentiment. A man couldn't say this out loud, because sentiment was supposed to be essentially womanish. How those old distinctions weary one, with their scientific data to prove that men surpass women in the senses of feeling and taste, while women have better sight and hearing, and so on through every conceivable mumbling of the human brain, forever harping on differences and emphasizing them, forever dwelling on sex distinctions and never on a common humanity."

"It was a dreadfully scientific age," she agreed, "a generation fearfully and wonderfully given over to statistics... and yet, how many dreamers there were!"

"Yes, but in the twentieth century, a young man dreamed dreams and saw visions at his own risk. While he dreamed of the brotherhood of man, his classmates with the corporation practice distanced him in the pursuit of position. While he led himself through the valley of the shadow of temptation, and feared no evil because of the Madonna vision in his soul, even the Madonnas preferred Lancelot and Tristram to Galahad. It wasn't an easy world for a man who wanted to keep faith with himself. It was a sham world of pretense—that world that lies drowned out there. And yet, I believe it was infinitely better than the lost Atlantis, better than the deluged planet of Noah, nobler and finer than the best civilization of which we have any trace. I never despaired of it, and yet as I grew older, I wondered if I wasn't foolish and mistaken in daring to hope and to dream."

"I know," she said again. "I think I did despair, for it seemed to me a dreadful, terrible world. I used to wonder how conscientious men and women could bring other human beings into it, to suffer and faint in the frantic struggle for the unrealities that made us miserable or happy. Consider how paltry they were! If we built a new house, we were infinitely more concerned to see that the contractor used pressed brick than we were to see that the construction of our own characters was sound. When we grew wealthy, we moved into houses of more stories; but how often did we say, 'Build thee more stately mansions, O my soul'? I had as clean and strong a heritage as you, but a different one. It's no use to comfort oneself with nice little aphorisms about the needle's eye and filthy wealth, and telling God's estimate of money from the kind of people He gives it to; I tell you biting poverty is a terrible thing, an unspeakable thing. It's a misfortune for a child to grow up under a sense of injustice. I used to have when I revolted against it all, when I hated with the blind, ferocious hate of a child, and I saw what David never saw—the righteous forsaken and his seed begging, not for bread, but a chance to earn his bread, and begging for it without being able to make fair terms. I saw my home sold under the sheriff's hammer, and my parents struggle all their lives because of the lack of money when they had everything else—nobility, character, truth, and education. My girlhood was a long series of going-withouts. Finally, I married a man who promised me everything. Ah, well, when has the Apple of Sodom failed to deceive the eye and undeceive the tongue? At least he did care for my voice, and through that I learned that all those years I'd carried in my own throat the golden notes to have altered everything, and I sang a little gladness into my parents' lives before they ended, thank God."

"How did you come to sing in opera?" Then he added, "Don't tell me if the recollection is unpleasant. I just wondered..."

"Because after—after things went wrong, I couldn't take his money. I knew how to sing, and I loved it; but even there, it was the same story of suspicion and jealousy, until it seemed to me that hate and fear ruled the world. I went to so many, many cities, but there was no beautiful city, and in all the country, I found no Arcady. I had money then, it's true; but the jingle of the dollar doesn't help the artist who sings, or paints, or writes, or plays, because God has put it into his soul to do this thing; at least, not after the very first, when it stands as a tangible assurance of success. The cities were 'cities of dreadful night,' and awful days; there were places that weren't hives, but styes of human beings, fighting for what they called life, to die, never having lived. Sometimes, I went into those jungles of civilization and sang to them. It was the only thing I could give them. It was there I got my lesson. I'd been singing 'All Tears,' when an old woman said in her feeble, trembling voice, 'Ye mun loe us, young leddy, to come to sic a place an' sing o' Him wha sa loed the warld that He sent His only begotten Son ta it, for it's only great loe that casts out fear, and this is a fearsome spot.'

Since then, I haven't hated anything, except wanton cruelty... and I know love rules when it is fearless, but that's very seldom. We were afraid to say, I love you, to anything more sensitive than a stray kitten, though the world has hungered and thirsted after the love we've feared to give even to our own children. And yet, just the love a man and woman may bear each other, unconsciously, is enough to transform the earth. We haven't been cross to each other; I don't believe we've spoken unkindly to anything this year."

He drew her into his arms. "Is it enough to regenerate the earth?"

"And keep it regenerated?" she echoed. "Do you know?"

"Do you remember telling me, long ago, of a story in which the woman said she'd never seen but one man whose mother she would be willing to be? And you said you felt this way about me? I was very proud of it then, but I am prouder of it now, since, feeling so, you cannot be unwilling to be the mother of my children. You aren't, are you?"

She nestled a little closer to him, and put her hand about his neck. He stooped and kissed it, and repeated his question.

"Unwilling? No; how could I be? I never dreaded maternity, except when—and that lasted such a little while. I don't dread it now. It seems to me it would be a blessed thing for us. But, Adam, Adam, tell me, for I've sat here all day asking myself, whether it's a blessed thing to be born, or a penalty that others pay."

"I think it'd be a blessing to be your son," he said steadily.

"And I think it'd be a blessing to be yours," she answered, "but he wouldn't be yours nor mine, but ours, plus everything in the past, truly the heir of all the ages, and the ages were full of pain and sorrow. Oh," she said passionately, "could you and I, loving him so, this son who is only our wish, could you and I, who know the weight of this weary world, bind it upon the shoulders of our baby boy and send him staggering down the centuries, the new Atlas of this old earth?"

They sat in silence for a long time. Then Adam said slowly, "I don't know, dearest; but I do know that you are tired and hungry, and I'm going to take you home."

They rose and disappeared through the gateway together.

XVII

Robin was shelling peas. Adam was reading her the story of their deluge. He paused, dissatisfied, and said impatiently, "I haven't described it at all. I've said all I had to say in less than a thousand words; one would think such a scene deserved a hundred thousand."

Robin smiled her inscrutable little smile. "I think you've done it very well. It isn't intended to be scientific. You haven't told all the strata that were turned skyward for a moment when that crevasse opened between us and the town. You'll find, if you turn to the first chapter of Genesis, that there's very little detail; but I'm sure that the one line, 'He made the stars also,' is as eloquent as a treatise on the nebular theory. If you were educated in geology and astronomy and so on, you'd load it down with an avalanche of scientific hypotheses, about which you'd really know nothing except by deduction, and over which future scientists would wrangle, part of them making you a god, and the rest proving you a fool. Be content to 'climb where Moses stood,' and produce literature."

"'Why should an author fret about The judgment of posterity? It is not, and it never was, And it, perhaps, may never be,'" quoted Adam, cynically. "I wonder what they'll call us, Robin, and who will lecture on my mistakes in seven or eight thousand years, and show how it never could've happened. Do you suppose there's anyone else on earth? Did the Atlantis people leave any literature behind them?"

Robin shook her head. "Who really knows? God hasn't left Himself without a witness, at any time. In some way, the story of creation has gone on and on. Every nation has its Eden and flood and Saviour. Esther was the first, I think, to have her wish granted 'even to the half of my kingdom,' and all the fairy stories since have borrowed the phrase. Cinderella is almost as old as Job; and the Irish, the Fenians, claim that Cadmus, the Phoenician, was one of their forebears. Wide as race distinctions were, there were strange and almost unaccountable similarities."

She went indoors to see to her baking, and coming back, went on with her work. Adam watched her silently for awhile, and then said curiously, "I wonder what you've missed most this year?"

"Pins and needles, and until Christmas, books and shoes and stockings and sugar and a cook-stove and a piano," answered Robin, promptly. "I can live without the opera and a telephone, but if you only knew how I cherish my stock of pins, and with what dread I look forward to the day when, like a poor white trash family I used to know, I'll refer to the needle. I used to think you could do anything with a pair of pliers and a bit of wire, but I tremble lest you may not be able to compass a needle." She looked up, and seeing Adam's troubled face said quickly, "Forgive me for being superficial; I'm so happy, I can't help it. What were you thinking of, Adam?"

He got up and walked away a few yards, and cut one of the long thick yucca leaves and stripped it down to the central spine, while he went on speaking to her. "I was thinking," he said, "of what Mill said about inventions, and how they hadn't helped the laboring man; that they'd neither decreased his number of working hours nor increased his comforts, and wondering whether it'd be better for a new race to find an electric light plant alongside their other plants, or whether they would better work out their own salvation, a little at a time, by main strength and awkwardness. I was thinking how strange our books would seem to men and women who knew nothing of the—the late earth." He held out to her what looked something like a needle threaded with coarse white linen thread. "Will your Majesty deign to look at this?"

She took it and looked at it

wonderingly, and then ran in and brought back a torn towel, and began mending it. "Why, it sews very well!" she said. "Who taught you that?"

"The mother of inventions, generally," he answered. "If you'd ever gone on the roundup, you might've had occasion for a needle and thread when there wasn't any nearer than a hundred miles. But you haven't answered my question."

"About inventions and so on? It seems to me you have to consider the raison d' etre of a people before you can tell the answer. What's the use of labor-saving inventions, if the time saved isn't of some great value? What's to be the chief end of man in a dispensation that has no bible, religious or otherwise, as a guide-post?"

"A very different end from the old one," answered Adam, half sternly. "Work shouldn't come to him as a curse, nor as his greatest blessing; at least, not hard, manual labor. There should be work enough to insure ease and comfort, and everyone should work freely and gladly. I'd educate the individual—he should be strong of body and keen of mind, and should feel that his talents were given him for use, not for concealment; he should use his hands, both of them, and find delight in their work. It's a beautiful world, it always was, but I don't know that the steam-engine brought men's souls closer together, or that the electric light let in any more radiance upon our minds, or that the great telescopes made heaven any nearer. It'd be a happier and a healthier world, if it was nothing more."

"Adam," she said abruptly, "if we had children, in what religious faith would you bring them up?"

"I don't know; I never thought about it very much," he answered honestly. "I have an ideal in my mind, but I can't explain it. I believe in one source of life, and therefore a common divinity."

Robin laughed quietly. "That's like the Hindu proverb, 'That which exists is one; sages call it variously.' That's been called pantheism or polytheism, and for that belief, the Jews expelled Baruch Benedict Spinoza from their synagogue. In our time, there was a very learned magazine published in its behalf, and I heard David Starr Jordan say no man could tell whether it was a mere jargon of words, meaningless and empty, or whether monism was the profoundest philosophy the world has ever known."

"I don't care what you call it," said Adam, stoutly. "I'm not afraid of names, and I don't know anything about any of those religions—pantheism, Spinozaism, or monism—but I do know I'd rather a child of mine saw God in everything than that he saw

God in nothing save his own narrow creed. I'd rather he was a pantheist than a Calvinist. Spinoza never burned anyone, did he, nor preached that hell was paved with infants' skulls?"

Robin clapped her hands and laughed again. "I beg your pardon for laughing," she said, "but the idea of Spinoza, the 'God-intoxicated man,' presiding over a sort of Spanish Inquisition is too absurd. If you only remembered anything about his gentle, retiring spirit and melancholy life—I think he was better known in our time than in his own, but his philosophy doesn't satisfy me. I'm willing to grant the identity of life, and its divine possibilities, but I cannot worship it as life itself, a mere manifestation of nature. I know that there's such a thing as living rock, and that it may be killed by a bolt of lightning as readily as a tree; but this doesn't make it any more worthy of worship than I am, and that is terribly unworthy. The rock and I are types of life, stages in the development of life, but for my child, there must be something better. For the child, I must lay hold on the everlasting life; I must find the rock that is higher than I am. I don't know of any manifestation of that life so great, so godlike, and so lovable as His who said, 'I am the way, the truth, and the life.'"

"But surely you don't believe in the

Immaculate Conception?" asked Adam, incredulously.

"I don't care anything about it, one way or the other. It's the immaculate life that concerns me. As you said yourself a few minutes ago, words cannot frighten me. Am I going to stand carping, 'Can any good come out of Nazareth?' What do I care if it comes out of Sodom and Gomorrah, if it is good?"

"But you surely don't believe in the miracles?" he asked.

"Surely I do, in some of them at least. I've seen a miracle or two myself. Besides, if you remember, the greatest proof He gave was that the gospel was preached to the poor. Buddha was a prince; he whom the Jews expected was to reign as a king. What a fall!—the gospel of hope and joy was brought to the children of Gibeon, the hewers of wood and drawers of water. The love of Christ has wrought greater miracles than He did. Look at the arena in Rome. Look at the whole countless army of martyrs. When Mrs. Booth died, the eighty thousand women that nightly walked the streets of London rebelled, and for once, the long aisles of brick and stone were swept clean of that awful arraignment of civilization. That was more of a miracle than satisfying three thousand souls with food. At least, it's enough of a miracle for me."

The tears came into her eyes, and she gathered up her pans and went into the house.

XVIII

They were sitting in the doorway together. Robin rested her chin in her hands and looked down the valley, the lines of perplexity deepening in her forehead.

"If only we had an angel with a sword, or without one, to tell us what to do," she said. "If only we were deeply religious with the old-fashioned orthodox religion, that would enable us to believe we were predestined not to be drowned—"

"Or if we believed in a personal God, without whom not a sparrow falleth, though the waters cover the face of the earth and blot out millions of His creatures," answered Adam. "After all, can we do better than follow the dictates of Nature?"

"Do you mean to look through Nature up to Nature's God?" answered Robin. "How can we worship any God as pitiless as Nature? Nature is strong, but is it our place to help her in her care for the single type? Perhaps we are the trilobites of a new Silurian period; well, trilobites were painfully common, but we need not be. Nature's laws are changeless, so we've been told with wearying insistence, but suppose you and I have wills as strong as Nature herself? Suppose we ask what she's done for the humanity of which we are a part, that she should demand fresh victims from us? Oh, I know; you'll tell me, 'What a piece of work is a man! How noble in reason! how infinite in faculty! in form and moving how express and admirable! in action how like an angel! in apprehension how like a god!'

"And I should answer, 'What is man, that thou art mindful of him? and the son of man that thou visitest him? For thou hast made him a little lower than the angels, and hast crowned him with glory and honor.'

"David or Hamlet, it comes to the same thing. Where are the crowns now, and how can we say Solomon wasn't right when he said the end of it all was vanity? What is Nature, and on what compulsion must we obey her? The imperative mandates of our own hearts? But what if our hearts are at war with our heads? Are we to follow no higher law than the blind instinct that moves the housefly? Or will we aspire to the indomitable soul of the mockingbirds that feed their young in captivity until they see they are prisoners for life, and then bring them poisonous spiders that they may die rather than live under such conditions? Should we give hostages to Nature, when she has given nothing to us?"

She was standing now and speaking with more vehemence than was typical for her. Adam caught her hands as she flung them out with a gesture full of scorn.

"Do you really think we have nothing? How many million lovers have envied Adam and Eve their paradise? This Nature against which you bring such a railing accusation, has she taken away more than she's given us? We had ambitions, you and I, but the way of ambition is full of weariness and disappointment and bitterness of spirit. We didn't expect peace and comfort and joy, but work and turmoil. Our slates were set with a sum—"

"Yes, a sum in vulgar fractions," answered Robin.

"Perhaps; it was a sum in which the unknown and unknowable quantity determined the result. We'd seen a good deal of what is called life—it's a good name to distinguish it from the death it so much resembles—and I'm half inclined to think Nature has been merciful."

"But if she was merciful to them," said Robin, quickly, "why were we excluded?"

"She gave them oblivion, the hereafter—whatever comes hereafter. She gave us each other. We were going to miss one another in the careers we had mapped out. We might have lost each other forever, or for eons of years. Nothing but a general breaking up of everything would ever have flung us into each other's arms. We were too interested in my career, my vast influence on the political situation, to consider any existence apart from the setting we'd chosen for the play. And after all, what was it, that career from which we hoped so much? I stood waiting my cue, ready to act my part in the farce or tragedy, whichever it turned out to be."

"I think it was more like a circus," said Robin.

"Very like a circus," he admitted with grim appreciation. "A circus in which no one knew whether he was to be a ringmaster or a clown. There were the financial tightrope walkers, and the social lion-tamers, and snake-charmers, and the political acrobats whose falls were unsoftened by any kind of network. There were heat and dust and discomfort, and weary, wretched animals looking out of cages at other weary, tortured animals, that were sometimes scarcely less insensitive than themselves. I know the program we had mapped out, the triumphal entry, the daring leaps, the cheers... but was it worthwhile? After all, does one care to be the champion bareback rider in life's arena? Nature swept away my sawdust ring, but she gave me heaven for a canopy, earth for an arena... you for a queen. At times, I'm disposed to take a fatalist view of the case, and think that God, or Nature, knew there was nothing more to be done with the earth, not so much because of its wickedness as on account of its stupidity and cruelty. All my plans had centered in a political career, and yet, how could a man touch politics and remain undefiled? Yes, I know there were honorable men in politics, but they were lonely, and they hated with an unspeakable hatred all the means that were used to keep them there. And there were any number of men who had been honorable once. When a man becomes possessed by the desire of place, his spine becomes elastic, and he stoops to things of which he'd believed himself incapable. I don't know what it is, but it weakens a man's moral fiber, and breaks down the tissues of his will, and gives him mental astigmatism. How dare I say I should've been any better than the rest?"

"Do you remember your address, a year ago Flag Day, and the old man with the little bronze button of the Civil War veteran, who stood in front and shook hands with you afterwards with tears running down his face? And the applause? Can you honestly say that you find 'to utter love more sweet than praise'? You've told me of your dream of a home, but Emerson said, 'not even a home in the heart of one we love can satisfy the awful soul that dwells in clay.' Can it satisfy you, who hoped and expected so much?"

He hesitated and did not reply at once.

"Are you sure you aren't making a virtue of necessity?" she asked a little bitterly.

"I think as much as anything," he said slowly, "that I was excusing myself for not having known all along that the real life is the one we could've made together. Principalities and powers and empires and republics have fallen. When God wants to regenerate the world, He begins with the family. Now I—" he emphasized with unspeakable scorn, "—I intended to begin with a different primary law. I could've made a good home, but I was intent on making an indifferent, honest congressman, or senator, or perhaps president. In a way, your home always meant a good deal of what I am trying to say. You always had someone on hand you were trying to make capable of great things by believing in them. You made us welcome, and were ready to listen to our troubles, our literary curiosities, our musical gems and our aspirations. Suppose I'd had sense enough to refuse the husks and choose—"

"Don't say it," she answered. "Don't say it, even if you mean it, for I should've sent you away, and have felt like reviling you for putting your hand to the plow and turning back. Your ambitions were the most attractive thing about you then. I hadn't pinned my faith on a primary law; I think it was government ownership that I regarded as the great regenerator. I'm glad if my home seemed 'homelike' to any one; it never reached my ideal, and when a woman's home isn't the hub of her universe... well, she takes to china painting, or gossip, or philanthropy; a man takes to poker or politics. I took to politics, secondhand. Personally and concretely, I abhorred the whole miserable farce, but abstractly, and as a means to an end which I greatly desired, I found it interesting. I admired you infinitely more than I liked you in those days, but I wouldn't have married you under any circumstances."

"Why?"

"First, because I didn't want to marry anyone; I didn't want to care that much. And secondly, because I wanted you to devote yourself to your country, and had you possessed a family, your devotion would've been divided. I don't see," she went on reflectively, "how you, who know so well how empty it all was, and how hopeless the endeavor to lift it an inch—I don't see how you can think anything would justify us in making it go on."

"But, on the other hand," he said, "are we justified in snuffing it all out? There was so much that was beautiful, and the possibilities   were   so   glorious! Sweetheart, I can't believe you love me if you think the world is all cold and dark. I believe now the one law it needs, or has ever needed, is love, the fulfilling of the law."

Robin shook her head, and there was a

pathetic quiver about her sensitive mouth. "Is it really? We've sung, "Tis love, it makes the world turn round,' but is it really? Would you give your world that one great principle as the whole of its code of laws?"

"Yes, I would," he answered sturdily. "I wouldn't revive a single law, not even the Ten Commandments or any of their variations. You have to read the statutes provided for unnamable crimes to understand just how bad mankind could be. I wouldn't bother my world with Draco, or Solon, or Justinian, or Coke, or Blackstone. I'd give it the code of Christ: 'Whatsoever ye would that men should do unto you, do ye even so unto them.' To love one's neighbor as oneself—isn't that code enough for any world? And I'd make the 'neighbor' include every simple creature."

She turned to him, her face radiant with love and trust.

"There's no difference between us in reality," she said. "You would found your political economy on the teachings of Christ, and I my religion. If we realize the unity of life, we must make our religion our law, and our law our religion. Sometimes, I think the hand of the Lord is in it, for surely, surely, there was never a nobler man on earth than you."

XIX

"Do you remember the name of that man we knew," asked Adam one day, "who wrote a book to prove the immortality of the body? He did prove that various people had lived up to two hundred years. If we were sure of that, we might get the earth very fairly started."

Robin laughed. "We aren't obviously growing any older," she said, "but we can hardly count on more than a hundred years each!"

"There's one thing you haven't taken into consideration," said Adam. "Our children would be several thousand years ahead of the original children of the Garden; they'd be further along than you and I in a good many ways."

"No," she said, "I haven't forgotten, but I don't know how much of a load they would bring with them into the world. We called it heredity, the Hindus called it karma, and, though it's a little different, educators called it the recapitulation theory."

Adam shook his head. "I understand heredity," he said, "but karma and recapitulation are too much for me."

"Karma is our heritage from former existences," she answered, "that may have been lived here or elsewhere. It's the sum of our past, good and bad. It's based on a belief in reincarnation, and it's the law that 'whatsoever a man soweth, that shall he also reap'. It's justice untempered by mercy, and it's at odds with the doctrine of alternate atonement, though one may believe it and worship Christ as the highest type of love the world has ever known. Naturally, it doesn't appeal to the people who are willing to let someone else bear the cross for them, and yet I've wondered—if we were sure we shouldn't gather figs from thistles, we should sow the thistles so freely.

"The recapitulation theory makes the child pass through the evolutionary stages of the nation or nations he represents. It has a kind of seven ages of man of its own, and brings him down through all phases—the savage, the hunter, the explorer, the conqueror, the builder, and so on. I don't pretend fully to understand it. I heard one of its most capable supporters once say, 'The soul of the German nation is in the German boy.' Heredity curses or blesses, sometimes both. Considering any of these theories, prospective parents might well hesitate."

"Which do you believe?" asked Adam,

curiously.

She reflected a moment. "A little of all three; not all of any of them. One would have to be a profound student to understand fully what their believers claim for them. Heredity plays strange freaks now and then. It's easier to account for Abraham Lincoln by the second theory than by either of the others. His shiftless, untidy mother and commonplace father don't explain such a soul as his; nor was there any reversion in his childhood to the original savage instincts that make children dismember grasshoppers—rather the reverse. I prefer to think that, like that other Deliverer, who was a man of sorrows and acquainted with grief, he came to do the will of his and our Father which art in heaven—came gladly, freely, knowing the end from the beginning."

Adam sat up suddenly and looked at her with startled eyes. "Then you think—you mean—you don't believe—surely you don't believe we have anything to do with our coming here?"

She smiled. "Surely I do. Our coming is sad enough when we do it voluntarily. It'd be quite intolerable to have existence thrust upon us. Besides, it seems blasphemous to me to believe that God's given to every human being the power to bestow an eternal existence. The responsibility is great enough when it's simply a matter of living so that noble souls may seek to be born of us, and undertaking to give them sound minds and bodies."

Adam looked unconvinced and troubled. "Where on earth did you get all that?" he asked.

"Well, it is, to my mind, only an elaboration of Descartes' 'I think, therefore I am.' I am presupposes that I have been, and will be. If you can't destroy one drop of water, you can't destroy me. If you drop the water on red-hot iron, it instantly becomes an imperceptible mist, the mere ghost of itself, but it'll ultimately become fluid again. It seems to me that the scientific fact gives a sound basis for the psychologic probability."

"But think of all the miserable human beings born daily. Do you think anyone would choose such surroundings?"

"You and I never wanted to go anywhere badly enough to crowd ourselves under the cow-catcher or upon the trucks, but there were those who did. We didn't want to see the parade badly enough to stand on the street corner for hours; but you worked your way through college, and we have both sat in the top gallery to hear 'Tannhäuser.' We were willing to put up with the whips and scorns, which is another way of saying the garlic and tobacco, for the sake of the music. In any event, the experiment was of brief duration. No one gets more than a fragment in an ordinary lifetime."

"If you think that," said Adam, "I can't see that there's any responsibility about it. We shouldn't thrust life on anyone."

"True," she assented. "Your position is unassailable, but still it seems to me the responsibility remains. In the first place, granting that my hypothesis is true, how can we tell whether to live is to gain? How do we know that the next generation would be better and stronger than we are? Moreover, I only give this to you as my idea. I don't say it's true; I believe it to be true, but I don't know anything whatsoever about it. I can't prove it, and it may be otherworldly rubbish. I rather imagine you think it is."

"Not exactly that," he said, coloring and laughing, "but certainly it's rather amazing when one hears it for the first time. I daresay I'll come to believe it, too. So far as I can see, you're about as unorthodox as I am."

"I have times of relapse," she said. "Then I think we're being tempted like the first Adam and Eve. They were commanded to multiply and reign. You and I wouldn't ask anything better, but as a rule, one's duty is not attractive. It seems to me just as likely that we're to prove that the lesson is learned, and that a man and woman may love each other unselfishly and nobly, foregoing their own desires to save others. Under the old dispensation, it was said, 'Greater love hath no man than this;' isn't it possible now that the greatest love is that which lays down its life untransmitted? If Christ could pray that the cup of suffering and death might pass from Him, dare we press the bitter drink of being to other lips?"

"Dare we dash the full goblet of joy and opportunity from them?" asked Adam, gravely.

"I wish I knew," she said. "I wish I knew!"

"Have you ever thought what it'll mean," he said, "if we adopt the other alternative? Have you thought of the desolation and loneliness of growing old and helpless and finally..."

He stopped, and she threw out her hands as if to ward off the thoughts he called before her.

"Oh, yes, yes, I have thought, and it's terrible. I keep remembering a picture I saw in the French Exhibit. It was of a man and a woman; the woman was dead, and he'd dug her grave, his broken sword lay at his side, and he'd wrapped her in his coat and begun to cover her over. He couldn't go on, and knelt, looking at her with a despair on his face that's haunted me ever since. The name, Manon Lescaut, meant nothing to me then, but the story of the picture was enough by itself. All last year, I kept seeing that terrible picture. Sometimes it was you, sometimes it was I, that dug the grave and went mad looking into it."

"I couldn't bury you," said Adam, grimly. "I'd carry you to the cliff and take you in my arms and jump. The sea is deep and cruel there."

"Sometimes..." she hesitated a moment, then went on, "sometimes I think that would be the best way for us now—I mean, if we decide we have no right to be happy in the old way; for I'd be afraid we couldn't always be strong."

"Very well," he answered. "When we decide, it'll be literally life or death."

XX

For a time, they busied themselves with different things about their little home, worked in the garden, and held a roundup of their stock so they could know the extent of their wealth; and because, in a life quite apart from human beings, animals came to take their place to a greater extent than might seem possible.

It was a very pleasant time. Everything seemed so gentle, so willing to be friends, and so certain of their goodwill.

"You used to be a Kipling fiend," said Adam one morning, when they had been salting the cattle and were resting before going home. "Didn't he write a Jungle tale about 'How Fear Came'? He ought to be here now, to write another to show how Fear might go."

"It seems to me he did," Robin answered, running her fingers through the short, curly forelock of a colt that stood placidly licking her hand. "I wonder that they don't remember longer, or perhaps they know that we think they're folks. Really, I think we ought to hold a reception once a week, so as to keep acquainted with our neighbors."

"You're an absurd child," he said, laughing; "but does that mean that you've decided to go on living?"

"I don't know," she said. "What did we determine? By the way, which side of this question are you on?"

"Both," he said decidedly.

"Oh! Then we can't do like those men Cooper told about—in 'The Pioneers,' wasn't it?—who argued and argued every night until at last they convinced each other, and then started in to argue it out again."

"No," he answered, "I rather think that we're answering ourselves rather than each other, anyhow. Robin, where was 'the land of Nod'?"

"That's one of the questions that I was sent to bed for asking a preacher who was visiting at our house, when I was about seven years old. They hurried me away before he had a chance to answer, so I never found out. But I know what you're thinking of, and I've thought of it, too. Perhaps there isn't any land of Nod, or any land at all. And I've thought, also, how it'd be if one of us died and left the other with little children. You might take my body and jump off the rock, but you couldn't take them, too, and you certainly couldn't leave them."

"I've thought of the risk to you," he said, "and felt that not even for the sake

of a child would I let you come so near
death."

She laughed a little. "That's really
funny," she said. "You must've been reading
Michelet; I never thought of that at all.
I'm very healthy and strong, and my habits
and clothes don't hamper my life nor
endanger that of another. There's next to
no risk, so far as that's
concerned—certainly none I wouldn't gladly
take. But I've dreaded afterwards, when the
child might fall ill and need help that we
couldn't give it."

"Because there are no doctors in the
world?" said Adam, with a touch of
cynicism. "I don't know that we aren't
better off without them. The greatest of
them confessed that it was guess-work. The
best doctors I ever knew were always trying
to make their patients live more simply,
take more exercise, and give nature a
chance; they never resorted to medicine
until there was nothing else to do. If all
the germs and microbes have gone with them,
the earth can stand the loss. The main
thing is to be born well, and when the body
is healthy and leads a natural life, while
it may know pain, it needn't be prey to
disease. Very few children had a heritage
worth having. It'd been bartered away. No
wonder we were taught to say, 'There is no
health in us.'"

"Do you remember Gannett's 'Not All

There'?" she asked soberly. "I'm not sure I can recall it, but it began this way:

"Something short in the making, Something lost on the way, As the little soul was taking Its path to the break of day.

"Only his mood or passion, But it twitched an atom back, And she for her gods of fashion Filched from the pilgrim's pack.

"The father did not mean it, The mother did not know, No human eye had seen it, But the little soul needed it so.

"Thro' the street there passed a cripple Maimed from before its birth; On the strange face gleamed a ripple Like a half dawn on the earth.

"It passed, and it awed the city As one not alive nor dead; Eyes looked and burned with pity. 'He is not all there,' they said.

"Not all! for part is behind it, Lying dropped on the way; That part—could two but find it, How welcome the end of day!"

For a long while neither spoke, then Robin went on. The colt had wandered back to its mother, and she sat with her hands clasped and her eyes looking far out to sea.

"I don't blame people for dreading the responsibility, nor even for shirking it, when I think of all the conditions we had to face. Men who thought they'd hedged their trades with so much skill that they'd banished competition, found that they'd only succeeded in bringing into the field the machine that banished them. And everywhere there was such ghastly poverty—poverty of body and brain and soul. We'd gone back to patrons and patronesses. Men or women didn't do anything with themselves anymore—they didn't sing or play, or give a reading, or exhibit a painting. They starved, or they performed or exhibited 'under the auspices of.' It's always been the same. Given a pure democracy, and demos reigns sooner or later. The shiftless go to the bottom, the thrifty to the top, and then, like the upper and lower millstones, they grind everything between them. Those below cry, 'Alms!' and those above respond, 'Generosity!,' and the voice that cries, 'Justice,' is stifled between. The stone that crushed from above and the rock that ground from below were very near, and men dreaded them, for when the grist is ground and flint strikes upon flint, the fire is at hand. Do you think I'm talking like a Populist campaign book? I only know what I saw, and what the poets have said. I wouldn't dare to be as radical as Lowell, nor as bitter as Tennyson, nor as savage as Carlyle, or Ruskin, or Hugo. We'd overcome the sharpness of death, but how could we hope for deliverance from the sharpness of living?"

"We've been delivered," said Adam,

slowly, "but you don't seem disposed to be the Miriam of this limited Israel."

"Well, no," answered Robin. "I'd like to believe that you and I were rewarded for our superhuman excellence by being saved when Pharaoh and his multitudes went under, but a somewhat wide acquaintance with other people forbids that. On the other hand, we can't have been left on account of our great badness. Truly, Adam, don't you feel sometimes as if you'd rather have died with the rest?"

He hesitated. The question was so unexpected, and so fraught with possibilities. She watched the struggle in his face and honored him for it. He put back a stray lock of hair and kissed her forehead before he answered.

"The streak of cowardice that we all have in us," he said finally, "the distrust of myself, and the doubt of all systems of life of which I know anything, prompts me to answer Yes; for I think even if we'd died, you and I'd still be together. I think sometimes we have been, in the past, but whether we have or not, I know we will be in the future. So while the mental part of me—which it seems to me is the weakest and most contemptible part of man, because it's always reasoning him out of what his soul tells him is true—while the mental part of me might find it easier to be dead than to know what we ought to do, everything else in me rejoices. I know that in the great plan we have a part, it seems to me a very happy and beautiful part. In all our world, there's no cause for anger or hatred or sin. There's friendliness and content and gentleness and love all around us; look up, dear, and see how near heaven seems."

But though she looked up, she saw only the light in his eyes.

XXI

Robin's music was a source of great delight to both of them.   There was such a sense of time, infinite and unlimited, that they ceased to be the hurrying mortals of earth.   The joy of life crept into their hearts, and they grew young with the new world.

One evening, they watched the full moon come up over the mountains.   She had been playing a few desultory airs, and looking up asked, "Who said, 'music is love in search of a word'?"

"If you don't know, I'm sure I don't," answered Adam, laughing.   "Do you know that you quote entirely too much?"

"Oh, yes," she said lightly.   "I always knew that if I ever break into print, the critics, supposing they ever deigned to notice me, would say, as they said of Lubbock's 'Beauties of Life,' that it wasn't a book, but a compendium of useful quotations.   But do you really dislike quoting?   I think it takes nearly as much originality to quote well as to invent."

"Oh, no!" he interposed.

"No?   Well, it seems so to me.   I think the thing first myself, that's original so far as I am concerned, though it may be old as the hills, and then it comes to me afterward, in a dozen ways, perhaps, as other people have said it. I realize that, in the kaleidoscope of life, the pattern before my mind's eye approximates that which others have seen. We don't say a man knows too many synonyms or antonyms, and I don't see much difference."

"I have a misty memory that quotation is said to be a confession of inferiority," answered Adam.

"That's Emerson," she said, laughing, "but he also said, 'genius borrows nobly,' and I'm willing to confess inferiority to a great many people; all that implies is that one should only quote well. If it wasn't that I'm not sure of the words, and that I can't verify them, I'd confound you with a citation from Disraeli."

"Go on," said Adam, lazily; "I don't mind being crushed."

"It's to the effect that people think that where there is no quotation, there must be great originality. Then he says, 'the greater part of our writers, in consequence, have become so original that no one cares to imitate them; and those who never quote are seldom quoted.' That's about it. Now are you answered?" She laughed gleefully. "It's delicious to disagree with you. I'd almost forgotten that it was possible."

He echoed her laugh with the carefree heartiness of a boy. "I'm going to make a riddle," he said. "Prepare yourself; this is the first conundrum of the new world. Why is it better to disagree than to differ?"

She made a little grimace. "It's a wonder the Sphinx doesn't rise from the other side of the world and eat you," she said with derision. "Anybody who loved anybody could answer such a poor little excuse for a riddle as that; besides, it sounds like an extract from somebody's 'First Easy Lessons in Rhetoric.' Don't you see that I can disagree with you, while I must differ from you? That is too disgracefully easy. Indeed, Adam, that riddle of yours brings back every doubt, for they say—scientists and -ologists and learned people, you know—that there's hope for delinquents and defectives, but none for degenerates, and that is an awfully degenerate joke."

"Play for me," he said, "and don't call names."

She lifted the bow and drew it across the strings in a series of cadences so wildly mournful that he shuddered. She put the bow down, and laid her hand upon the strings to still them. In the old days, she had been given to sudden changes of mood, but of late she had been almost serene.

"What is it?" he asked gently.

"Oh, nothing—everything! I was thinking of another thing which those wise ones said," she answered, with more bitterness than she had shown for many months. "That word 'degenerate' brought it back. You know birds are a very low order of being, a branch of the reptile family, in truth, and I've heard people say that musicians are generally lacking in something. They either have no moral or financial sense, and cannot be bound by ordinary rules. And I am musical to the very tips of my fingers. It's as if I could hear the song of the silence—I feel its vibrations like those of a great organ."

She paced up and down, her hands behind her head and the moonlight shining on her upturned, troubled face.

"There's another scientific fact you forget," he said.

She stopped to listen, and he went on.

"When a race has run its course, nature cries 'finished,' and nothing can alter its fate. It wasn't just the merciless onslaughts of the white man alone that exterminated the buffalo. They died, and none came to take their places. They vanished, less on account of man's cruelty than by reason of their own sterility. Degenerates or regenerates, can't we leave the decision with a power that forever builds or destroys, in accordance with a law we don't understand, a higher law that comes from the source of all law, whatever that source may be? Don't think anymore, but play for me. In spite of my lecture, I'll quote, too; my mother used to sing a hymn that went like this—'I'd soar and touch the heavenly strings, And vie with Gabriel while he sings,'—Do you know it?"

She began the old tune, "Ariel," and then wandered on, playing many airs that brought back forgotten days. Adam threw himself down on the grass to listen, half jealously, for she seemed to forget everything. She had seated herself on a great boulder, and, leaning back against it, her eyes looking into the blue depths above her, she played on and on. The old tunes were merged in new ones, and the high sustained notes of the Cavalleria, the subtle minor of Wagner, the exquisite sweetness of Beethoven and Schubert filled the moonlit canyon, and still she played on, melodies new to Adam, intoxicating, full of a wild ecstasy that filled his very soul, and thrilled through him until he felt all power of resistance swept away. Every other desire in the world was lost in the supreme and overwhelming longing to gather her to his heart and hold her there forever. The very air was steeped in melody. The full majestic chords rose and melted in unison with the high, exquisitely sweet notes, and throbbed their life away.

She held the bow suspended a moment, then very softly, half unconsciously, played a dreamy lullaby, and laid the violin down in her lap.

Adam took her and it into his arms.

"Be careful, put it down gently," she said faintly, "it's your soul and mine. Do you not know the secret of Antonio Stradivari, of all the great makers of violins? Ah, they solved our riddle, Love, ages ago. Do you not remember the story of Jacob Steiner, and how he spent days and days in the woods, selecting the trees for his violins, and how the spirits of the trees revenged themselves by telling him of their ruined lives until he went mad?"

"But there was no madness in this music," Adam answered, "except, except—"

"The supreme, sublime madness of love? Do you not know, surely you do, that every perfect violin is as much man and woman as you and I? The back of the violin is made from the timber of the female tree, the belly of the male tree. The harmony depends on their vibrations, as they clasp each other in an embrace as real—"

"As this," he cried, drawing her closer and bending his handsome head until their lips met. "Sweet, must I envy that violin?"

He felt her heart beating wildly against his own, their arms closed around each other convulsively. The sweetness of the music-laden, flower-scented air filled his senses.

"God! How I love you!" he said.

A frightened look came into her eyes, and she struggled for a moment, futilely.

"Let me go," she whispered. "Let me go!"

"Do you want me to?" he answered, studying her face in the moonlight.

"No," she said. "No, never again, but, oh, Adam!"

XXII

Adam had to go to the cane-fields across the range, and one of the calves needed Robin's ministrations, so she could not go with him. He started before the stars were set, so that he might be back before night, and returned twice to kiss her before he finally got away.

Left with the long day ahead of her, restless and lonely, she gave the small house a thorough cleaning. She had finished her dusting and was rearranging the furniture when she shoved back the long chest and struck the framework of the window with a little too much force. It was enough to jar a rusty key from its place above the casement, and it dropped upon the chest with a kind of ominous clink as it struck the lock and fell upon the floor. She picked it up and looked at it curiously, and then, kneeling, fitted it into the lock.

"I wonder," she mused, "what I'll set free if I open this box; is it Pandora's? But there was nothing left in hers but hope, and that's all we need. How happy we'd be if we dared to hope!"

She turned the key with a hard twist,

and the hasp shot from its place. The chest was nearly empty, there being just one parcel in it. This was done up carefully in a square of linen, pinned here and there.

On the bottom of the chest were several folds of white paper.

Very slowly, she lifted out the parcel and opened it. The treasure was a gown; it was of a heavy, satiny weave of linen, very yellow and creased. The bodice was made without sleeves or neck, and the skirt was a kind of kilt-plaited affair; the whole effect was Greek, and, simple as it was, seemed beautiful to Robin after her year of dark, utilitarian clothing. There was white underwear, and even white stockings, and a pair of slippers.

Robin drew a long breath of delight and, laying all her finery upon the table, placed the irons over the tripod that she might smooth the wrinkles out, and set about making the necessary alterations at once. She worked rapidly in spite of her excitement, but the hours slipped away.

"I must try it on," she said, "before Adam comes; there'll be plenty of time, and then I'll put it away until—"

Shroud or wedding-gown? She did not finish the sentence. She dressed slowly; but when she had finished, she was startled to see that the image in the glass was so much fairer than she had ever thought herself. Suddenly she discovered, with something like a pang, that there was no belt, and hurried back to the chest to look again.

As she twitched out the remaining layer of paper in her eagerness, a long white satin ribbon dropped from it, and a little heap of fine muslin lay on the floor of the chest. She caught up the ribbon with an exclamation of delight and adjusted it with trembling fingers. Her flushed cheeks and radiant eyes, the long heavy braid of hair, her round white arms and shoulders, made her a vision of delight indeed.

She sat down by the chest to inspect its last secret. As she took up the pile of lace and muslin, her heart seemed to stop beating for a moment.

She had forgotten. Only the hands of the prospective mother could have fashioned such dainty garments as these. Everywhere the eternal question. All her perplexities had fallen from her in the joy of dressing herself as Adam's bride—whether Adam saw her not—but the great problem of life confronted her still.

She put the tiny garments down on the chest, closed now, having given up its mystery, its hope of the world, and knelt by it, touching them with loving, reverent fingers until the tears blinded her. She gathered up the clothes and kissed them as she had never kissed Adam, as she had never kissed anything in her life.

After awhile, the tears ceased to flow,

and a gracious calmness stole over her, and then the slumber of a child.

She did not hear Adam, nor see him, until he passed the window and stood in the doorway, the sunset glow behind him. Then she started to her feet, her arms closing instinctively over the tiny garments she had gathered to her breast as she stepped back, her face flushing and paling all in a moment.

He stood as if he dared not move lest the vision vanish, but heart and soul looked out of his eyes.

"Eve," he said, "Eve!"

She turned, and he sprang toward her with an eager cry of joy.

"Eve," he repeated, "Eve, my love, my soul! You've decided; you're going to be my wife. Oh, don't torture yourself or me any longer with doubts that didn't enter the mind of God Almighty when He made us what we are. You are my world, dearer than life, more necessary than the air we breathe. We're only one being, separated God knows how long, but united now forever. Nothing can part us again."

He stopped and held out his arms to her. He had taken her into their shelter very often, but now he wanted her to come to him and nestle against his heart of her own will.

She took a single step, stretching out her arms to him with a gesture of infinite trust and abandon.   The long sheer dress fluttered down to the floor, and lay between them.

They stood still, as if frozen.

"Do you dare cross it?" she said, and hid her face in her hands.

He stooped and picked it up, and looked at it as a man might look at the soul of something of which he had never seen the body.   He had a sense of his own strength, the glory of his manhood, and a vision of his weakness.

She watched him breathlessly.

He put the garment down on the table and smoothed it out gently.   In his face was the combined look of a man who sees the cradle and the coffin of his firstborn.

She went and stood beside him, touching the dress timidly.   He covered her hand with his own.

"My wife," he said, "we know all there is to say, all there is to risk.   We must do what is right.   I'm going now to set everything free.   It's nearly sundown; you'll meet me at the rock in half an hour. If we give each other our right hands, we will fear no evil, not though we walk through the valley of the shadow of death, for the love in our hearts is deathless, and though the sun sets, it will rise upon another shore.   Death is only an incident, but life is eternal."

"We couldn't choose differently?"   And

though she spoke with the upward inflection, it was not a question.

"No, it would be quite impossible for either of us to desire what the other did not. And much as we love each other, we'll know we have loved our race and honored God first in our decision. To live, if we live, not for ourselves alone, but for the good of our kind; to renounce love, the unspeakable gift, if need be, for the sake of what seems right to us."

"And if I give you my left hand—?"

The sudden flash of light in his eyes half blinded her. He took both her hands in his and looked deep into her beautiful, unfathomable eyes.

"Then the morning stars will sing together, and all the sons of God will shout for joy."

The sun dropped lower and lower over the high sharp peaks at the west, covering their white summits with a flood of golden glory. The sullen roar of the ocean seemed hushed, and across its wide expanse, the last beams of the setting sun made radiant pathways of crimson and gold. A lark, far up in the heavens, sang its few clear notes as it hastened homeward. Far away on the mountainside, the cattle lay placidly, and a mare whinnied to her colt. The air was soft and warm and drowsy with the scent of many flowers, the sounds of nestling birds, the drone of an insect here and there, the cheerful call of the crickets.

Adam stood by the rock and waited for her. She came toward him, all the light of the world seeming to fall upon her and circle her in a halo that transformed her white draperies, and glistened like a million gems in the sparse grass about her feet.

They exchanged no greeting, but stood and looked into each other's eyes, grave and sweet with the exaltation of their purpose. And, standing so, they clasped hands, and the word they spoke was the same, for by searching, they had found God.

Jennifer Hurt is the mother of two, a son and a daughter, and the grandmother of four, three grandsons and a granddaughter.

In her lifetime, she has worked as teacher, a librarian, a bookstore clerk, and an English tutor. Thanks to the original The Master-Knot of Human Fate, books are in her blood.

She lives near Fulton, New York.